FERAL PRINCE

QURILIXEN LORDS: A QURILIXEN WORLD NOVEL

MICHELLE M. PILLOW

MICHELLEPILLOW.COM

Feral Prince (Qurilixen Lords)

Feral Prince © copyright 2021 by Michelle M. Pillow

First Printing August 19, 2021

Published by The Raven Books LLC

ISBN-13: 978-1-62501-277-7

ABOUT FERAL PRINCE

Prince Roderic hates the diplomacy demanded of his position as a cat-shifter royal. As the son of a diplomat, he's all too familiar with the treaty surrounding the Federation military occupation, Shelter City. The shifters can't simply ask them to leave, or they'd risk retaliation. Discretion is the key, which includes not getting caught mingling with those under Federation protection. So crossing paths with the beautiful Justina is a mistake waiting to happen. She's frustrating and rash and doesn't mind drawing attention to herself. But, as fate would have it, she's also the one woman he wants to call his own.

For decades they have dealt with lies and deceit, but when the humanoid population under the

Federation's control begins hunting shifters out of desperation, he knows things have gone too far. It's time to drive the Federation off his planet once and for all, even if that means losing his one chance at true love.

PRAISE FOR QURILIXEN LORDS

"Filled with intrigue and adventure, Dragon Prince: A Qurilixen World Novel is an exciting new spinoff in a rich and intricate universe. Michelle Pillow creates characters to cheer for, to hope with, while building worlds that are portals for the imagination. Truly, Ms. Pillow is a master of futuristic fantasy."

Yasmine Galenorn, NY Times, Publishers Weekly, & USA TODAY Bestseller

"Michelle Pillow weaves a fantastical tale of dragon shifters, full of rich world-building, action and adventure, along with a sexy love story. This entire series is not to be missed!"

Bianca D'Arc, USA TODAY Bestseller

"Sometimes you just need to gobble up the insane goodness that is dragons, and Michelle has been aiding in that addiction for fifteen years."

Eve Langlais, NY Times & USA TODAY Bestseller

"A wonderfully sexy tale filled with romance and dragon-shifters that draws you in from the first page and doesn't let go. The Qurilixen Lords series is one you don't want to miss!"

Mina Carter, NY Times & USA TODAY Bestseller

The Playful Prince
The Bound Prince
The Rogue Prince
The Pirate Prince

Qurilixen Lords
Dragon Prince
Marked Prince
Feral Prince
Fire Prince
Her Lawless Prince
Poisoned Prince
Cursed Dragon

Captured by a Dragon-Shifter Series
Determined Prince
Rebellious Prince
Stranded with the Cajun
Hunted by the Dragon
Mischievous Prince
Headstrong Prince

Space Lords Series

His Frost Maiden
His Fire Maiden
His Metal Maiden
His Earth Maiden
His Woodland Maiden

Dynasty Lords Series

Seduction of the Phoenix
Temptation of the Butterfly

Having trouble finding the books?
Updated Buy Links Here

To learn more about the Qurilixen World series of
books and to stay up to date on the latest book list
visit www.MichellePillow.com

AUTHOR UPDATES

Join the Reader Club Mailing List to stay informed about new books, sales, contests and preorders!

michellepillow.com/author-updates

To my husband, John, and the adventure we are on every day.

THE METALLIC SMELL OF BLOOD PERMEATED THE forest, the scent unmistakable against the darker tones of earth and trees. It filled Roderic's nostrils and drove him from a deep sleep onto all fours. Already shifted into cougar form, his senses were heightened. He stood alert, ready to fight as he focused on his surroundings.

Roderic missed the forest of his childhood. Things seemed more straightforward in youth, or perhaps he'd been fiercer and ready to take on the universes.

Roderic thought of the Federation's presence. No, it had been simpler. Now everything was complicated.

The forest smelled like blood, enough to wake

him but thankfully not a bloodbath. Not shifter blood. Humanoid? Cysgodian?

Sacred cats!

Roderic had fallen asleep away from the Var palace where he lived but near the Federation Military's stronghold of Shelter City. By agreement, the Federation had a right to occupy the valley. Some shifters would say that decision was the single worst in Qurilixian history. But what else could they do? A virus had wiped out nearly all of the Cysgodian population and destroyed their homeworld. They needed a place to recover, and Qurilixen's unique atmosphere aided in promoting health. Scientists said it had to do with the radiation from their three suns, particularly the one blue sun unique to their planet. They determined the virus caused no threat to shifters, and at the time, they were the Cysgod aliens' only hope of survival. What else could they do? Turn away hundreds in need?

And it worked. The visitors survived.

Over thirty years had passed, and they continued to survive.

Barely.

Sure, the virus hadn't killed the new residents since their arrival, but the poverty and neglect might. And there was nothing the shifters could (legally) do about it.

The dilapidated city was a blight to the planet of Qurilixen and an embarrassment to the ruling shifter families of Draig and Var. What was supposed to be a temporary shelter for the Cysgodian off-worlders had turned into a standoff between the Federation and Qurilixian people, with the Cysgodians stuck in the middle.

When the elders had agreed to partner with the Federation to save the Cysgodians, they couldn't have known the course of events that would unfurl. Before Shelter City, shifters had kept the Federation off their planet, and they'd kept out of the Federation Alliance.

Though the residents weren't supposed to venture past the city's borders, some had been caught outside city limits. Roderic didn't blame them. Families starved, and poverty had become a way of life. It was no wonder they had begun to rebel.

Roderic focused his senses as he tried to track the blood. At least it was faint. That was something. No giant battlefield. No massacre.

Someone still might need his help.

His paws hit the soft forest floor as he navigated

through the trees. Individual leaves large enough to cover his head created a thick canopy above, and their fallen brethren spread beneath him in a decaying carpet to pad his journey. Some of the trunks had grown as wide as a small spacecraft in this part of the forest. Their bark looked as if it had boiled to the surface to grow in a bubbly texture. The Var left this part of the forest undisturbed. The Federation would gladly cut down all the trees and sell them off-world to the highest bidder. They would strip the land, mine all the ore, and leave desolation in their wake.

Roderic had no proof of these plans, but neither was he an idiot. They'd done it before to other planets. Qurilixen was too far out into the Y quadrant to do much good as a strategic military base in the multiple universes.

He paused, listening to his surroundings. A faint shuffle caught his attention, but he couldn't distinguish between humanoid footsteps and wildlife.

He took a deep breath. Definitely not shifter blood—so that ruled out the Var marsh farmers or Cysgodians hunting shifters. Some in Shelter City had become convinced shifter blood held the key to immortality. Others were just hungry and desperate enough to consider trying shifters in their cat and dragon forms. So far, neither plan had been success-ful, thank the gods.

The blood could be from Cysgodians who failed at hunting shifters. Soft flesh was no match for claws and talons.

Or Cysgodians running from the city.

Or human captives escaping Federation imprisonment. Two women had recently been rescued. They were now married to dragon-shifter princes and under Draig protection. Was this another prisoner? Fiora and Salena had a missing triplet sister.

The smell of blood became stronger. Roderic focused on the scent, and all thoughts of the Federa-tion politics melted from his mind as he tracked the source. With the thought of another woman running from danger, his primal instincts took over. Women were meant to be protected.

The same properties that made Qurilixen optimal for health had created a medical anomaly in which most of the shifters were born male. Though more females had been born in his generation than those that came before, it was still only a tiny few compared to the males. Most women came from off-world and tended to be delicate in nature compared to shifters—no fangs or claws to protect themselves.

Thus, it became accepted that women needed protection.

Shifter women hated that assessment, as they'd proven themselves as fierce as any man.

Truth be told, most alien women hated that assessment as well—at least all the wives who had married into the royal families.

His head lowered as he stalked through the brush, ready for danger. Every nerve in his body prickled with awareness. Roderic leaped nearly twelve feet to stand on top of a fallen trunk. His claws dug into the bubbly texture of the bark to keep from slipping on the mossy overgrowth. It gave him a better vantage point over his surroundings.

"Oh, no, no, no, don't do that. Wake up, lady. I won't carry you."

He stopped to listen to the woman's frantic voice. The tone was soft as if she was aware someone might be listening.

"I told you I can't be out here." She sounded vaguely familiar, but it was too difficult to place where he might have heard her. "They'll notice I'm gone when they send the drones to do the heat counts. But these woods aren't safe either. I can't leave you like this."

Roderic jumped down and took a quiet step, careful where he placed his paws.

"Maybe I can conceal you in the city, but all of my spots are," she hesitated and grumbled, "not any place you'd want to wake up. And if you don't wake up, I can't have a dead body stinking up my best hides. The scanners would detect the smell."

Roderic took another step, then another. He was close.

"Hey, you, wake up." A rhythmic slap preluded a light moan.

His heartbeat sped. The animal inside him enjoyed the mystery of the hunt.

Light danced through the canopy above. Roderic focused his shifter vision between two trees to where a woman crouched with her back toward him. Her gown had been patched with mismatched material, some of which were faded in spots. The condition of the clothing instantly told him she lived in Shelter City. Even the Var who chose to live feral in the forest, drinking nef all night and passing out by their stills, were cared for better than the Cysgodians.

The woman's red hair had been piled messily on top of her head only to have wisps of curls escape. The striped discoloration of the skin along her temples clearly revealed she was a Cysgodian woman. For a moment, Roderic forgot why he was there. Beyond the blood hid the scent of a woman, and that one tease to his senses caused his entire body to stiffen in surprise.

Who was she? Surely, he would have remembered that scent.

The woman lifted her hand to the side, and Roderic detected crimson staining her fingers. The trace was faint, and he would have missed it if he hadn't been so focused on her.

"Don't make me hit you," the woman warned. Her arm began to lower as if to strike.

Roderic let a low growl erupt from the back of his throat in warning. The woman shot to her feet and spun toward him. Blood smeared her sleeve and dotted her shoulder. He studied her for injury as she swayed on her feet. She stumbled to the side.

Roderic's gaze met the woman's frightened one. He inhaled sharply and the growl locked in his throat. He felt his claws dig into the earth. The hunter inside him had stirred to track the blood and didn't appreciate being restrained now that he'd discovered the source.

Animal instinct fought with man's reason. He should never let the predator take over. In shifted form, it was too easy to lose himself to the wild.

Roderic forced his gaze to where the woman had been kneeling. He found the source of the blood. Fiora slumped against the base of a tree. Though she looked like her sister, Salena, this had to be Fiora. That triplet was prone to nosebleeds when her psychic visions became too much. The blood smeared her face and even caused her long brown hair to cling to her cheek. Though that didn't make sense. Since Fiora had mated with Jaxx, that bond had calmed her visions, and she was able to better control them.

Fiora had the ability to see the future and had prevented a liquor still explosion in Shelter City that would have killed everyone. She also was unable to lie when asked a question. It made her both invaluable and dangerous. In contrast, her sister Salena's gift was that she could pull the truth from anyone like a human lie detector. One question was all it took, and confessions would pour out. The missing triplet could read people's intentions or something like that. He wasn't exactly sure. It's why the Federation had imprisoned Fiora and chased Salena. General Sten had wanted control over that power. Though both were now under Draig protection.

What was Fiora doing here? Alone? In Var territory?

Where was her husband, Prince Jaxx?

Was this woman trying to kidnap her? Bring her back to the Federation? Such a gift to her overlords would put her in excellent standing. Though he disapproved, he couldn't say he blamed her.

Something smacked his shoulder, drawing his attention back to the redhead. She searched the ground with her hands while keeping her eyes on him.

"Go. Get!" The woman threw a stick at him. He leaned to the side so it missed his head. "Leave us alone!"

She continued looking for ammo and produced another stick.

Roderic gave a low warning growl, telling her to stop. Though she clearly didn't speak his language as she launched another wooden missile at him.

"I know you can understand me," she said. "You're one of those animal-men. Leave us alone. We don't want any trouble."

She threw a stick at him, then instantly another. Roderic dodged the first, but the second poked him the cheek close to his eye. He grumbled more than growled at the discomfort.

The redhead lifted a larger stick and held it like a sword as she put herself between him and Fiora. "No food here, shifter."

Food? Gross.

Roderic would have laughed if Fiora's situation didn't look so dire. The redhead bumped Fiora's leg and caused her to fall to the side into the thick underbrush. Fiora did nothing to break her fall.

Realizing he would learn nothing from her in his cat form, he leashed the cougar and pushed the man to the surface. His bones cracked as he took on his human form. It was an old pain he ignored.

The redhead gasped and trembled. Her stick sword dipped down as she tried pointing it at him.

Fur retracted into flesh. He remained on all fours as fingernails replaced claws. Dirt from his night sleeping outside marred his skin. Even as the human took over, he kept his keen sense of hearing and sight as he assured himself that they were alone in this section of the forest.

When he could finally speak to her in the Old Star language, he slowly stood. "Who are you?"

The redhead took a deep breath as if to steady herself and lifted the sword with determination. "I knew you were one of them. Stay back. I don't want any trouble."

He couldn't see Fiora's face hidden by thick brush, but he heard the soft rustle of plant life when she breathed. She was alive.

The redhead's eyes darted down his body. Roderic didn't care that he was naked. It's not like his body absorbed clothes each time he shifted. Though his nudity did seem to distract the woman.

"Your name," he insisted.

"You first." The woman's tone wasn't as shaky as he'd expected it to be as she stared a little too long at his hips.

"Prince Roderic of the Var." Sacred cats, why had he used his title? Was he trying to impress her? Scare her? The cougar tried to surge to the surface with impulses of his own.

She studied his face as if trying to ascertain if he told the truth. "You don't look like a prince."

"What do princes look like?" he countered.

"Less feral. I imagined most would be clothed." The stick sword lowered by small degrees.

"Does my nakedness alarm you?"

The woman laughed. "Seriously? You can well suspect where I'm from. Someone is running the streets naked at least once a fortnight. Usually screaming during a psychotic break, but there you have it. Such is life."

"Your turn." Roderic was glad her eyes had moved away from his hips. With that face and her slightly humorless laugh, any man would start to show sexual interest, and his blood already raced from stalking her through the forest.

"Justina, not a princess of the Cysgodian." Her tone mocked his formal title, albeit slightly. She lowered the stick and pointed at Fiora. "Do you know who she is?"

Roderic nodded. "Fiora. What are you doing with her?"

Justina relaxed a little more. "Getting her royal stupidness out of the city. Since you know her, I give the responsibility to you. I've done all I can. When she wakes up, tell her to stay out of Shelter City. It's no place for outsiders."

Justina kept the stick but backed away from him to create a clear path between him and the fallen Draig princess.

"Don't hurt her," Justina warned. "Not that I can do more than threaten to avenge her, but just don't. She asked I take her this way before she passed out. I have to assume she knew what she was doing."

Justina turned to leave.

"Wait." He took several steps after her causing

13

her to lift the stick again. She pointed at his chest. He slowed his walk and stopped near the tip of her weapon. "What happened to her?"

Justina lowered the stick. The tip skated down his chest and stomach before dropping to the side. The strange caress made it difficult to concentrate. Hot liquid attraction burned through him.

"I don't know. When I found her, or rather she found me, she was rambling about someone being dead and asked me to get her out of the city so she could go for help. Against my better judgment, I did. I couldn't leave her in the streets, and I couldn't hide her. She was making too much noise. One of the Sweeper borgs would have scooped her up, and it's no secret what will happen if your people are caught with mine. So here we are. And now, I must get back. There is a curfew, and they are heat counting my quadrant. If they don't find me there, they'll search my home, and it's impossible to get the smell of sweeper exhaust out of furniture."

"Sweepers don't have exhaust," he countered.

"Huh, funnily enough, I don't have furniture." Justina turned to leave.

"Wait. How can I find you?" Roderic didn't want to watch her go, even though he knew he had no reason to make her stay. She was in enough danger just being outside the city limits. The Federation put people to death for less—not that General Sten would admit to as much.

"You don't find me. Ever." Justina's lip curled at the side. "This is the end of our story, prince. We're written in two very different books."

He kept part of his attention focused on Fiora's continued breathing.

"Do you know the way back?" he asked, still not wanting Justina to leave. "Or you can come with me to the palace. I can make arrangements for you to be taken off—"

"No. You should know better than to offer an escape. If General Sten catches us breaking the deal between the Federation and shifters, he'll retaliate in a way that would be bad for both our people." Justina swung the stick at a thick patch of underbrush before stepping through it. "I'll be fine. I marked my path, or rather it's been marked long ago. Tend to your responsibilities. Goodbye, feral prince."

Roderic wanted to follow Justina but resisted. Fiora needed him. He kneeled on the ground next to her and eased her out of the brush. He placed his hand around her neck, feeling her steady pulse against his fingers. New blood trickled from her nose over the dried. Her eyelids did not flutter open, but at least she breathed.

Fiora was dressed for travel in tight black pants and a fitted brown shirt. A long patched jacket covered the clothes to help her blend into Shelter City. The nondescript garments and the fact she was with a Cysgodian woman meant she most likely had been venturing into the city. If she was in the city, Jaxx should have been with her.

Roderic lifted her into his arms and began carrying her over the uneven terrain toward the Var palace. He couldn't think of a better plan. They were in the middle of the forest. No one expected him to return home, so no one would think to come looking to offer assistance. The cat-shifter palace expected two shiploads of alien dignitaries, which was one reason he'd disappeared to sleep in the forest. Unlike his parents and younger brother, Roderic did not have the patience for such gatherings.

At best, Jaxx would be in the air trying to find his wife. The dragon-shifter would have better luck spotting them on an open path, away from the dense canopies. If that happened, Jaxx could fly her to safety. Otherwise, Roderic needed to get Fiora to the palace and into a medical booth. From there, he could communicate with Jaxx's parents and tell them he had Fiora and Jaxx was missing. Not everyone in their respective families knew about the secret relief trips into the city, so alerting the Draig palace would be a mistake.

Seeing the fallen tree, he took a running start and leaped on top of the trunk. The jarring movement bounced Fiora, and her arm slipped from her chest to dangle. Roderic lowered her to the trunk to readjust her body. The second her back touched the slippery bark, she flailed. The action took him by surprise. A scream erupted from her throat, and she swung violently. The movement propelled her off the trunk, and she slid over the side.

Roderic fisted the first thing his hand touched to stop her descent. Claws erupted from his fingers out of reflex, and he stabbed them into the trunk to prevent them from falling. His knee slipped, and the bark scraped his naked stomach and jarred his manhood. He grunted in pain.

Holding their weight with his clawed hand, he realized he had a fistful of her hair in the other. Fiora flung and screamed. She grabbed at his hold on her hair.

"Fiora, it's Roderic," he pleaded. "I'm trying to keep you from falling."

She kept flinging her body.

"It's Roderic," he insisted. "Jaxx's friend."

At Jaxx's name, she settled some and twisted to try and look up at him.

"Roderic?" She gasped. "Roderic! All the voices. We have to find him."

"Fiora, I'm slipping. I have to pull you up or lower you to the ground." Roderic's fingers ached where the claws strained.

"We have to find Jaxx," Fiora insisted. "I can't feel him. All the voices."

"I'm sorry, my lady, I have to lower you. Watch your landing." He eased the hold on her hair. The strands slipped through his fist.

Fiora dropped to the ground with a loud thud. Roderic thrust away from the trunk and retracted his claws. He landed away from Fiora.

"I can't. Too many voices." Fiora crawled toward him, her limbs shaking. "We have to find him. I'm sorry, I have to look into your future. I have to concentrate."

Worry filled him at her panic. Even though he was a dragon, Jaxx had been one of his closest friends since childhood, like a brother.

"Fiora, what happened to Jaxx?" Roderic demanded. Fiora would be compelled to answer, and that was better than having her peek into his future. He did not want to know what was coming. It would be like reading the last chapter of a story before the middle.

He thought of Justina.

"This is the end of our story, prince. We're written in two very different books."

A foolish part of him hoped that wasn't true.

"I don't know." Fiora stopped short of touching his naked chest. She glanced down as if realizing he was unclothed and averted her gaze back to his.

"What do you know?" Roderic asked. "Tell me everything."

"We were in the city to see Yevgen. Jaxx and Payton had retrieved bionic limbs for him when they stopped that explosion in the city. They traded the limbs for monitoring the city for information," Fiora said.

Roderic nodded. "I remember."

"Yevgen detected the guy they call Yellow Shirt with one of the stolen food simulators." In answering his question, her words became less frantic.

Roderic and his cousin Payton had helped Jaxx smuggle the food simulators onto the planet with the help of space pirates. They had hidden them near the city and had planned on setting them up in the surrounding woods so that an underground network of collaborators in the city could sneak food to those in need. Before they could set them up, they'd been stolen.

"We went to the city to get a read on Yellow Shirt's future timeline so I could hopefully lead Jaxx to where the units were hidden," she said.

"And did you get a read on his timeline?" Roderic asked.

Fiora nodded. "Yes. I was near Yellow Shirt so I could focus on him. Proximity makes the future sight stronger." She closed her eyes and began shaking her head. "I saw him with a simulator. He was giving it to one of the military guys in exchange for a bag. I couldn't see inside because, the second the bag opened, the timeline exploded with hundreds of voices. It was like before I mated to Jaxx. All the timelines screaming for attention. I can't see my own future, so I can't see his..."

Her voice caught.

"I can't feel him, Roderic. Why can't I feel him? He's my everything, my life. We're supposed to be connected forever," Fiora whispered. She pressed her shaking hand to her chest. "I have no heart without him."

Pain formed a hard rock in his stomach. Roderic

could guess the answer. There was only one reason he could think of that Fiora would not be able to feel her shifter husband. When shifters fully mated, it was for life, and that life force became infused with their partner. If Fiora couldn't detect that life force, then there might not be a force to feel.

It was entirely possible Jaxx was dead.

"We have to go back to the city," Fiora said. "The woman, Justina, she'll be able to show us where she found me. Jaxx was there—"

"You can't be in the city when you're like this." Roderic gestured at her bloody nose. Her gaze went to his fingertips. Bruises had formed from his claws digging into the tree to hold his weight. "I can't allow—"

"Can't allow?" Fiora's expression hardened. "I don't need your permission. Either you come with me, or I'll go by myself. And I can't lie, so you know I'll do it."

Roderic wanted to protest, but what could he say? Jaxx was her mate. To a shifter, that meant more than a lifetime of friendship. Jaxx would want him to take care of his wife.

"Jaxx told me of your friendship. He loves you, and I know you love him. He told me if I ever needed help, all I had to do was ask you. Please,

Roderic. Help me." Fiora's eyes teared. "It hurts to breathe without him."

"Wait here. Try to rest and focus your thoughts. I'm going to run for clothes, and then we'll sneak into the city." Roderic stood. "I promise we'll find him."

He hoped it was a promise he'd be able to keep.

2

Justina tucked the front of her skirt into her belt to free her legs for the run through the forest toward Shelter City. The sound of her feet created a steady rhythm. She concentrated on that sound to keep her nausea from erupting into something worse. The stitch in her side didn't slow her steps. It couldn't. Not if she wanted to make it back before they discovered she was missing.

She didn't have time to worry about the woman she'd left behind in the forest with the naked shifter. For all her talk, the sight of him turning from cat to man had rendered her speechless. Though they had seen the dragon-shifters flying in the sky and blowing fire, she had only heard of the cats. She'd never seen one in animal form.

Fiora was kind, but she wasn't from Shelter City. Justina could do nothing more for her. The universes were a cruel place. In the end, everyone took a chance just by being alive.

And no one cared.

When a virus wiped out a planet, not many off-worlders wanted to go near the infected. They expressed concern but did not open their homes. So the Federation used saving them as an example of their benevolence.

When a society stopped being useful, people conveniently forgot about it. No one cared what happened to them after relocation. In their minds, the Cysgodians were saved, and life could carry on. She doubted her former world was anything more than a lesson in a virologist's upload.

Justina turned her steps toward a tree near the city limits. She tried to slow but ended up crashing into the trunk to stop her momentum. Her body slid to the ground as she gasped for breath.

Just a few seconds. That's all she could wait. Just a few deep breaths.

If they discovered she'd slipped past the borders, everything she worked so hard for would be lost.

Justina forced herself to stand. With a quick

glance around to ensure she was alone, she counted twelve giant steps away from the tree and then kneeled to search the forest floor. Her fingers found a rugged seam along the ground. Natural litter was attached to a trap door with the spacecraft maintenance adhesive she'd received in a trade.

As she lifted a trap door to reveal a tunnel in the red earth, she didn't give herself time to think about what she was doing. Thinking would only lead to panic—panic that the top might collapse and bury her alive, panic that a wild forest creature might be hiding in the dark hole, panic that someone might see her exit.

Justina crawled headfirst into the hole and let the trap door slam shut over her. Instantly, she was cast into blackness. It had taken her years to dig the tunnel, and there was only enough room to crawl. The stifling smell of dirt could choke a person if they stayed down there too long. Her heavy breath in the narrow space kept the silence from collapsing in on her.

Just like when she ran, she listened to the sound of her hands and bare knees shuffling over the dirt. She had to keep her mind off what she was doing. With the front of her skirt hiked up, her legs were exposed. Hard dirt chunks bit into her skin. She moved faster. At intervals, her fingers would brush past one of the support beams. Some were wood, and others were made from bent metal tubes. Tree roots slowed her progress, so she turned on her side to squirm her body past them.

This wasn't too bad, or so she assured herself. Leading Fiora into the woods had been the real danger. Anyone could have seen them escaping the city. But what else could she do? Justina had seen the woman several times with her husband. They tried to disguise themselves but weren't as stealthy as they thought. A person could put on tattered clothing and rub mud on their faces, but that didn't change how they moved. Like throwing a pebble into water, there was something almost indescribable about the way they rippled the flow of the city.

Luckily for the strangers, most of the residents of Shelter City knew to keep to their own. The last thing you wanted was to draw the attention of the Sweeper borgs, or worse, the Federation soldiers.

As the city slowly decayed for over thirty space years, so did the pretenses that started with it. When they first arrived, it was all welcomes and altruism. And, slowly, as the eyes of the universes turned away, those niceties dropped. Food rations dwindled. Homes began deteriorating.

Justina's skirt snagged on a protrusion, instantly wedging her on her side between tree roots. She inhaled sharply. Particles of dirt filled her lungs, causing her to cough violently. All efforts to distract her mind fled as fear came raging in. The space was too tight to reach her legs. She clawed at the tunnel floor, trying to gain leverage. She pulled on her dress, but it only seemed to make things worse as the material ripped. The darkness made it impossible to gauge the whole situation.

"Calm your thoughts, Justina," she whispered. "This is not how you end. This is not how you end. This is not the darkness of death."

The roots must have grown just enough to make the trip more challenging. She pushed against the ground, rocking her hips to reverse course. Dirt clung to her sweaty skin. She heard it trickling off the walls to mark her movements. Inch by slow inch, she squirmed until the material loosened its hold. Then, tugging the edge of her skirt from the belt, she tried pulling the material through the opening first. Finally, after much work, she was able to slip her legs through.

Justina pushed her foot against a root to propel

herself forward. There was no time to catch her breath, and she didn't want to be in the tunnel any longer than necessary. She hooked her skirt around her arm and again turned her thoughts to the sound her hands and knees made against the ground.

Justina crawled so fast in the darkness she didn't realize she had hit the end until she literally smacked into it with the back of her hand. Pain radiated down her finger.

"Blasted piece of space rock…" She bit her lip and forced herself to remain on task.

Justina felt for the metal of the trap door in the ceiling. Slowly, she pushed up, listening beyond the exit. Even though it was evening, a light came from outside. On a planet with three suns, they only had surface darkness once a year. She continued up until she could peek along the ground. There were no feet, but she didn't expect there would be.

The edge of her home butted up against the metal barrier linking her house to a neighbor's. There wasn't much space, if any, between buildings, and the haphazard way the town had been constructed left plenty of little nooks and crannies to hide in throughout the city. Luckily, her newest neighbors didn't know about their shared alcove. The only one who had seen it was Starrs, and he'd been smacked so hard by a Sweeper borg that he didn't say much of anything anymore. He forgot to eat if she didn't remind him.

The biggest threat came from the sky. Since the heat-seeking drones flew overhead, she didn't want to get caught crawling out of the earth. Loud clangs carried on the air with a mixture of voices and the softer burr of engines. A faint beep sounded. The drones were near.

Justina crawled out of the hole and slammed the trap door shut. She messed up the dirt around the opening, making it blend. Her finger had begun to bruise where she'd jammed it in the tunnel, but there was little time to worry about it.

Prying back the edge of the metal barrier, she slipped through to the other side and ran down the narrow alley to her home.

Starrs' broad shoulders blocked her path. Age had begun to creep along his weathered face and revealed itself on his steady hands, the years tallied in scars and wrinkles. She imagined those same lines on her father's face if he had lived. His hair was longer than hers, pulled back at the nape of his neck to hang in a tangled mess. He made a strange noise whenever she tried to cut it. She had known him most of her life, ever since what was left of his family sat down next to hers on the transport ship to Qurilixen.

"Have they counted us yet?" Justina asked.

Starrs grabbed her by the arm and began to pull her toward his house. She noticed he'd taken one of her metal side panels and placed it along the front of his home. When she looked at her house, the panel had been replaced with stone from his wall. It used to clang and vibrate when the wind cut across it, keeping her up at night, and was less insulated than the stone.

"Starrs, you should keep your stone," Justina said, thinking that is what he meant to show her. He waved his hand and continued to pull her.

She looked up at the sky. Patched canvas flapped overhead, giving shade from the constant daylight of the planet. The soft red glow reflected on the material in two long flashes. A few seconds later, a low tone sounded in warning to empty the dirt street in front of their homes. Everyone else in their sector had gone inside.

"We need..." Realizing Starrs would not let her go, she changed course to get him into his house. She quickened her step, forcing him inside.

Not surprisingly, he'd dismantled his furniture, and it sat in neat stacks around the open room of his home. He'd rebuilt all of it into something new only to disassemble it again.

"Help." Starrs pointed toward a pile.

"I can't help you with parts right now," Justina said. "But in the morning, I'll come back."

"Him." Starrs kept pointing.

"Him?" Justina frowned. "Help him?"

Starrs didn't move.

Frowning, she went to look behind the pile of disassembled furniture he'd used to create a barrier between a man and the door.

Fiora's husband.

Though he wore local clothes, she knew his unconscious face beneath the splattering of mud. She thought of the shifter in the forest. There was no time to get this fallen man to him.

"What happened?" Justina touched his face, feeling the heat of his skin. The man lived. She lifted his arm and dropped it, hoping to wake him. He didn't respond as his hand landed on his face. "Why did you bring him here? You knew the count is tonight."

"Help." Starrs lowered his hand to gesture at a bloody wound on the shifter's side.

"Help him," Justina finished for Starrs. She

could hardly yell at him when she'd taken the same risk to save Fiora.

Justina looked at the ceiling. The warning tone was closer. There was no time to move the shifter to another location. Thankfully, he wasn't in his animal form.

Her skirt was already ripped from the tree roots, and she tore off a long strip. Starrs helped her turn the man so they could bind his wound. When they finished, she said, "Lay on top of him. Match your body as close as you can to hide him from the scans and don't move. Hopefully, your biometrics will disguise his. I'll sneak back as soon as I can. We'll stuff him down the tunnel until the census is over."

Starrs nodded.

Fear knotted Justina's stomach. The plan counted on the drones not working to full capacity. She didn't want to leave the unconscious man with her friend. If the heat scan realized there were two bodies inside the home instead of one, they'd investigate. Starrs was of no importance to the Federation, so they had no reason to keep him alive. He'd become an example of what happened when you broke the law.

Her heart beat rapidly. Why had these shifter natives come to the city? They didn't belong here.

They could leave anytime they wanted, back home to their palaces and decontaminators and spaceships.

Shelter City was *her* home. These were *her* people. The Cysgodians couldn't leave, couldn't escape. They had nowhere to go.

She hesitated. Maybe if she yelled and ran through the streets, the drones would follow her. But then what? They'd only come back to finish the count. Starrs already had the man in his home. How long would he lie still waiting for Justina to return?

Justina rushed from Starrs' home. Red lights flashed overhead. The drones were close.

She hit the palm of her hand against her door near the top edge. The vibration unlatched it. She watched red lights flash over Starrs' roof as she stepped inside her home. The door hung open, and she waited inside the doorway.

The red light flashed over Starrs' home a second time.

Blast it all!

It flashed a third time.

A fourth.

One of the drones lowered and began to fly inside Starrs' home.

"We are many," Justina yelled, stepping to the

edge of her door frame. She waved her hands wildly. "We do not need to stand for this tyranny. We do not need to climb the mountain to partake of the riches. Declare me your queen, and I will rise up amongst you dirt monsters."

The drones redirected their attention, flying toward her. They buzzed in warning. She saw a few of her neighbors quickly glance out to see what was happening. None joined in her madness.

"There is no need to steal my living heat. You, my jealous metal discs, may dine with us." Justina knew she sounded mentally unbalanced. She also knew this was about to hurt. Now that she had the drones' attention, she stumbled a few steps beyond her door and lifted her hands over her head. They were programmed to focus on the most significant disturbance. "I—"

The drones beeped in warning and flew toward her. She closed her eyes. A stun blast hit her stomach, sending her flying backward. Before she hit the ground, metal arms extended from two of the drones and clasped around her wrists. The sudden imprisonment jerked her from her fall and changed the trajectory of her body. The motion caused one of her shoulders to pop, and she cried out in pain. Seconds later, two more drone arms snagged her ankles from behind and lifted her from the ground. She hung by her limbs, facing the earth.

What else could she have done?

Starrs was the only family she had left.

Her skirt had snagged with one of her ankles, and the material fluttered in the breeze. It did little to protect her legs from exposure. With her hips dangling, the weight of her body added pressure on her dislocated shoulder. Pain radiated like fire, but her body wouldn't respond to fight after the stun they'd given her.

Not that she could struggle for freedom as they lifted her from the ground.

Justina watched the dirt of her street disappear as the drones lifted her into the air, high above her home. The city became a mash of walkways and rusted roofs and strips of canvas, pieced together to shelter the poor. Other districts not expecting a heat count were lively, people moving through the streets like caged animals through chutes.

Her heart thundered in her chest. As much as she wanted them to release her injured arm, she knew she would never survive the fall. The higher they climbed, the colder the air became. It stung her thighs and nipped her nose and cheeks. Her eyes blurred from tears, and she whimpered in fright.

The drones turned, carrying her toward the cliff-side that created the edge of town. Above the Cysgo-dians, along the ridge, were evenly spaced buildings. Unlike the city below, the structures looked just as they had the first day she arrived. That is where the Federation soldiers lived.

Justina saw the impression of people standing amongst the barracks, watching her transport as she flew overhead. She hoped they took her there for a light scolding before releasing her back into the city.

It wasn't to be. The drones lifted her higher.

Lording over everything, a rectangular stone facility stretched the entire length of the city. Metal arches created patterns along the top. Though she'd been there for decades, it was a view she barely saw from her place on the valley floor. That is where General Sten lived. Prisoners who entered those doors were rarely heard from again.

She'd saved Starrs for the moment. That's all that mattered. Hopefully, she bought him enough time to hide the shifter in the tunnel before they finished the count.

That thought didn't stop the pain in her arm. The drones dipped and turned. Though they flew in unison, the motion bounced her body, and she cried out.

The drones carried her along the high facility before coming to the entrance. Now they were on top of the cliff, the ground was closer. It did not give her comfort. They flashed a series of coded lights to command a door to open before flying her inside.

3

Escorting a Draig princess around Shelter City would never have been Roderic's choice, especially one prone to psychic visions and bleeding from her nose. Jaxx liked to joke that he was tenth in line for the throne, after his cousins and uncles, and if they ever tried to place a crown on his head, he'd simply fly away. Still, a prince was a prince. If anything happened to Fiora, the Draig people would hold him responsible. Wars on his planet had started for much less and had lasted for centuries.

Yes, there was peace now, a treaty that only started with his generation and the betrothal agreement made between Princess Grace of the Draig and his cousin Korbin when they were born. Though he'd never been to battle, he had spent his entire life hearing the stories from his elders. In some—*albeit perverse*—way, shifters could thank Shelter City for their lasting peace. No one wanted to start two wars so close to home. The arranged marriage had not happened, and some were using that as an excuse to create discontent. Though long dead, his grandfather, King Attor, still had followers who hated dragon-shifters, just as the Draig had factions that hated cat-shifters.

"What are you thinking?" Fiora whispered.

They were on the edge of the city, about to slip into the passing crowd. Already the smell from below curled his nose. Personal decontaminators were not freely supplied in the city.

"That it is foolish to bring you here," Roderic answered at length as he laced his boots. He'd carried her through the forest in his shifted form on his back, which had been much faster than running at her stumbling human speed. Though finding Jaxx would be easier in his animal form, he couldn't risk it, not even half-shifted. If anyone saw him like that, it would be much worse than if they saw two humans dressed like locals sneaking in. It would be proof they were breaking the rules by entering the Federation-protected city.

"And?" Fiora prompted.

"Jaxx has been a close friend since we were children. He will never forgive me if anything happens to you. And I will never forgive myself."

"If we find that Jaxx is..." Her breath caught. "If we find anything bad has happened to my husband, it won't matter if I'm killed in Shelter City. I'll be dead anyway, and it will not be you who killed me. So I relieve you of that burden."

Roderic took in her determined expression. Dark circles had formed under her narrowed eyes, and he knew she tried to block the many futures bombarding her mind. The way Jaxx explained it, she only gained control over the visions when their mated bond had calmed the psychic ability.

"You're staring at me."

Roderic sighed. "Your nose is beginning to bleed again."

She swiped at it with the back of her hand. "Your shirt is too clean."

"Focus on my future if that will help you keep the voices calm, just..." He grabbed a handful of dirt and rubbed it over his chest. "I don't want to know my fate unless it can help Jaxx."

"You would be one of the rare few who doesn't want answers." Fiora touched his arm. "Thank you for this."

He nodded. "We'll find him."

"I really wish you had my curse for only being able to speak the truth." The pain radiating from her became palpable. "What gods would give me this gift to see everything except those things related to my future?"

He had no answer for that.

Usually, Roderic would jump down a steep incline to get below, but Fiora didn't have his shifter abilities and would be injured in the fall.

"Lower me down." Fiora sat on the edge of the cliff and held out her hands. The smoothed rock face made it difficult for Cysgodians to scale the side to escape, which created an effective barrier.

Roderic tilted his head and listened to the sound of the crowd passing below. He kneeled on the ground before taking her by the wrists. Fiora nodded before pushing herself off the ledge. Her body slid down the rock face. Roderic maneuvered onto his stomach to lower her as far as he could down the incline.

"Ready," Fiora said.

He let go, and she dropped behind the rusted wall of a metal structure.

Roderic pushed his body over the side and

landed on his feet next to her. "Are you well, my lady?"

She nodded.

"Keep your head down and follow me. I'm taking you to Yevgen. You'll be safe there, and he can tell me where to search for Justina."

He didn't give her time to respond before walking along the structure to squeeze between two buildings. The walls swayed as if the only thing holding them upright were the strands of rope strung between the rooftops. Small holes lined the rusted metal where it had popped free of the bolts.

"This place..." Fiora whispered with a slight sound of disdain. "No one should have to live like this. We can't let this continue."

Roderic paused near the opening and didn't answer. He concentrated on listening to passing footsteps moving over wooden sidewalks and pounding on dirt roads. The steady *clank-clank* of canvas rivets struck a metal pole as it fluttered overhead in the breeze. Beyond that, the sound of voices created a constant hum that was difficult to sift through, even with his shifter hearing. A vendor shouted over the noise as he sold patches of material.

Two young boys ran past, laughing and

screaming insults at each other. The sight caused his chest to tighten as he thought of his friend.

"They need to take care before they—" Fiora began.

A loud crash rang out followed by a scream of pain.

"Too late," she finished. "Go. Now. Everyone's distracted."

Roderic slipped from between the buildings. He glanced down the road to where a crowd gathered. One of the boys helped his crying friend to his feet and supported him as he limped.

Fiora hobbled for a few steps and inhaled a sharp breath. Roderic grabbed hold of her arm in concern to steady her.

"It's not broken, but he'll be feeling that for weeks," Fiora said. Her stride righted itself as if she'd disconnected from the boy.

Wood and metal planks created walkways through the city, glued into place with dried mud, though most people didn't bother to use them unless it had rained. He kept one ear on Fiora's steps and the other on the crowd around them as he navigated through the streets as fast as he could.

"A crust of bread?" A woman straightened her

arms and joined her hands before striking a man across the face. He tumbled into the street. She kicked him several times and then stood over him, yelling. "It's going to take more than that to lift these skirts!"

As the man laid on the ground holding his stomach, the woman stole the piece of bread and shoved it in her mouth as she walked away. A couple of the onlookers laughed, but most just ignored the fray as commonplace.

Roderic turned down a narrow alleyway off the main roadway to cut across the city. Instantly, shopkeepers came from their homes to show their wares. Fiora made a weak noise of discomfort at the bombardment of people.

"Extra rations," a woman offered. Her gray hair had been sheered along the sides and left long around the crown. She waved a loose fist so they could hear the soft clank of ration chips. "One stone."

"You should give them back to your sister," Fiora said, flinching as if an unseen hand tried to slap her. "Or her children will be forced to steal, and one will lose an arm as punishment."

"She caught you, Gren," a toothless man laughed.

"Are you calling me a thief? I run an honest business," Gren protested.

"Yes, you're a thief," Fiora answered bluntly. "And you cheat at games."

Gren drew back her arm, ready to swing. Roderic stepped in front of Fiora and made a low sound of warning in the back of his throat. The woman thought better of the assault and waved her hand in dismissal instead. "I can see why your man hits you."

Roderic could guess what she meant by the insult. Dried blood stained Fiora's face, and she looked like she'd been punched in both eyes.

The toothless man lifted a flap on his canvas bag and patted it without fully revealing the contents. "Recreation?"

"No. I doubt you have chandoo," Fiora answered. "It's the only thing that helps."

Roderic frowned at her reference to the dangerous drug.

"Metal scrap? I swear they're not stolen," a man in dusty brown offered. He looked as if he'd been sleeping in the dirt.

"No." Fiora pressed her hand to her head and closed her eyes. Fresh blood dripped from her nose. "Please stop talking."

Roderic swept Fiora into his arms, cradling her as he carried her swiftly through the alleyway. He charged toward everyone who tried to step in front of them. "Clear a path!"

"Why can't I feel him?" Fiora whispered, grabbing hold of his shirt. "I see everyone else. There are too many timelines."

"Try to block them out. Why don't you concentrate on me?" Roderic suggested. "You'll probably see lazy days sleeping in a forest. Meditate on that."

"I can't look at you," Fiora answered his unintentional question. "Your timeline is full of too much pain and heartache that you have no wish for me to tell you about."

Roderic stumbled at her admission.

"Heartache?" The word barely left his mouth, but it was enough to trigger an answer.

Fiora pointed at the sky. "There it comes."

Roderic looked up, expecting to see one of the dragon-shifters, but the skies were empty. He carried her out of the alleyway into a walkway. "Can you guide us to Yevgen's without being seen?"

Fiora didn't lift her head from his shoulder. "Stop."

Roderic stopped walking. They stood, not moving for several seconds.

"Go," Fiora said, still not looking around.

Roderic hurried across the street.

"Wait here."

Roderic stopped again.

Fiora pushed at his shoulder. "Set me down."

He obeyed her commands without question.

"A woman with the red scarf. She'll turn and look at us. When she looks away, go." Fiora wiped her hand under her nose as she looked at the ground.

Roderic glanced toward the sky, wondering what Fiora had seen, but it was still empty.

He found the red scarf on a woman pulling a cart filled with worn canvas. Her cart hit a rut in the road, and a wheel became lodged. Tired eyes met his for a long moment as if wishing him to help her before she jerked the cart free and moved on.

"Walk." Roderic guided Fiora by her elbow into an opening between two metal structures. He had her walk first so he could be on the outside should anyone come after them. The narrow path forced them to turn sideways. From the outside, it didn't look like it led anywhere.

Their contact, Yevgen, never left his secret home. In many ways, it seemed as if he'd built the entryway to ensure he couldn't get out. Fiora turned a narrow corner, remaining sideways, as she went under the metal sheeting into darkness. Roderic's eyes adjusted to the dark to watch her.

"Look down, or you'll trip," Fiora said.

Roderic's toe struck a step.

Fiora knocked softly before pushing a hinged board to open Yevgen's door. Blue light flashed from within. The fact Yevgen had constructed his home between the exteriors of other buildings kept it hidden from any census the Federation would do. For this reason, the interior was a series of sharp angles.

"Yevgen, it's Fiora and Roderic." Fiora turned toward the source of blue light, a wall of monitors showing different views of the city in various resolutions. In the center was a picture of the Federation's complex on top of the cliffside where General Sten resided. She leaned close to the monitors, searching them for signs of Jaxx.

Movement sounded from another part of the home. Yevgen lived alone and valued his privacy—even if his spying said he didn't appreciate the same for anyone else. Though he couldn't see it, Roderic knew the sound of Yevgen pulling himself into a sling. Next, metal caster wheels rolled along the ceiling as the cyborg appeared.

"Princess Fiora, back so soon?" Yevgen's arms

reached through the sides of the sling as he hung from the ceiling. The cyborg hadn't yet replaced his legs with the ones Payton and Jaxx had scavenged for him.

"Jaxx is missing," Roderic said. Yevgen's mechanical eyes focused on him. "She can't feel him."

Roderic's face appeared on a monitor as Yevgen looked at him.

"Is Princess Payton with you?" Yevgen asked as a picture of Roderic's cousin appeared where his had been. The cyborg lacked a sense of urgency. Though Payton found him charming, Roderic was less amused.

"Not this time," Roderic answered.

"Zoom there," Fiora said, tapping a screen.

Yevgen turned to where she pointed. The image widened. What looked like a foot poking out from behind a stack of crates ended up being a piece of broken wood.

"When you say you can't feel him, do you mean he has broken your heart and left you?" Yevgen asked.

Fiora stiffened at the comment.

"Dragons mate for life," Roderic said, his tone low with warning. Fiora was already upset. Yevgen would only make that worse. "There is no such thing as leaving a mate."

"Ah, but not so for the cats." Yevgen chuckled. "Isn't that right, my furry friend?"

Roderic did not want to get into half mates and full-mates with a cyborg.

"I have been reading about shifters. Fascinating species, you are. Even though female births are traditionally rare in your kind, your great King Attor married over a hundred wives." Yevgen looked at Roderic expectantly.

"Have you seen Jaxx?" Roderic asked.

"Did King Attor have a hundred wives?" Yevgen countered. The cyborg thrived on knowledge, and apparently, this was the topic of trade he wanted in exchange for searching.

"A hundred and sixty-three half mates, I believe," Roderic said. In truth, Attor was a bit of a family embarrassment. There were some who followed his teachings, but they no longer had a political foothold. "He died before I was born. He had strong beliefs that we no longer pursue."

Yevgen nodded and turned toward Fiora, "I have not seen Jaxx since you left here with him."

"Do you have recordings? Can you track where we were when Jaxx was taken? We were close to that woman Justina, the one who stands on the crate and screams to those passing in the street." Fiora did not take her eyes from the screens as she desperately searched.

Yevgen turned to Roderic. "Did Attor marry all the shifter women? The other shifters did not complain when no wives were left?"

"I thought we had already traded for bringing the bionic legs to you?" Roderic said.

"Jaxx and Payton brought the legs. It is they who must make the request." As Yevgen said the names, Payton's picture came up on the screen and held for a few seconds before going back to a view of the city. The cyborg had a strange fascination with his cousin.

"Attor's wives were all off-worlders. He, and others like him, believed in emotional detachment and that life mates were the lot of lower society, for those who could not afford more than one wife or had no opportunity to negotiate with aliens for them." Roderic nodded toward the screens. "Can you track Jaxx?"

The screens began to flicker as Yevgen filtered through the cityscape. The cyborg kept his gaze fixed on Roderic.

"Of what possible use are my grandfather's

marital beliefs?" Roderic asked. "It has nothing to do with this city."

"Please, just tell him whatever he wants," Fiora begged. "Tell him why Attor had so many wives, or how it worked, or anything."

Roderic sighed, giving Yevgen what he wanted. He watched the screens as he spoke. "King Attor and some of the elders believed that for a Var man to prove himself, he had to have prowess in the bedroom as well as on the field of battle. We were at war then, so this was a point of great importance, and they believed there was a practicality to it. A cat-shifter can only have one life mate and, if that mate dies, that is it. But if a half mate dies, there are others to take her place. Since shifters are naturally —*stop*."

Roderic pointed at a screen showing two children chasing a third through an alleyway. They threw balls of mud at each other.

"Naturally?" Yevgen's sling rolled closer to Roderic.

"Go back," Roderic ordered.

Yevgen frowned but took the screen back to a woman screaming at an empty street.

Roderic's breath caught as he confirmed it was Justina.

"Yes, her," Fiora said. "Zoom in."

"Naturally?" Yevgen prompted, wanting his information.

Roderic stared at Justina's face as the image filled the screen. The sound was still off, so he couldn't hear her words. He thought of their meeting in the forest. "Feral."

"Naturally feral?" Yevgen's footage stopped searching. "But I was led to believe the Var were highly cultured and advanced."

"You've heard of the nef stills of the marsh farmers?" Roderic asked. "When the Var drink nef, it helps leash the animal inside when it comes to sexual prowess. Attor encouraged his men to consume it on a regular basis so that their thoughts would never be consumed by one woman. Besides a few elders, no one follows those ways. I don't know why you care to learn about them. I promise to answer your questions about it—*later*—if you help us find Jaxx."

"Your promise trade is acceptable," Yevgen answered. He turned toward the screens. "I do not have footage of his disappearance."

"What is Justina saying?" Fiora asked.

The sound instantly came on, and Justina's voice shouted into the enclosed space. "We are many. We do not need to stand for this tyranny. We do not need to climb the mountain to partake of the riches. Declare me your queen, and I will rise up amongst you dirt monsters."

Roderic frowned. This was not the impression he had when meeting her in the forest. She waved her hands wildly. "Her mind...it's not all there?"

Fiora pressed her palms to her temples. Tears filled her eyes.

"There is no need to steal my living heat. You, my jealous metal—" The recording stopped and was replaced by one of Justina standing on a crate, still yelling. "The thief has struck again, raining terror on those who would suppress—"

"I have been tracking her for some time and have many hours of her rants," Yevgen admitted, as the recording paused and the image flickered. "Though her words sometimes contradict themselves, I am not convinced her mind is as muddled as she pretends it to be. She keeps her ear to the mud."

"She is dirty?" Roderic didn't understand what the cyborg meant.

"She knows much about the city," Yevgen corrected. "I wish to recruit her as one of my runners, but I have found it difficult to lure women into my home. Perhaps, you, Princess Fiora, could convince her to meet with me."

"What?" Fiora blinked heavily and kept her hands pressed to her temples as she tucked her chin to her chest.

"Justina's newest favorite has been to warn citizens about a thief terrorizing the Federation. She is convinced such brazen acts will bring the wrath of General Sten down on the city. I've heard the same rumors but have concluded the thief is nothing more than the beginning of a local myth."

"—us," the recording continued. "Why do we sit idly by when one faces the many on our behalf? We should join forces. Show our strength so that the tyranny of Shelter City—" A ball of mud smacked Justina in the chest, knocking her over. The screen changed to yet another image of the woman screaming into the streets. "Life does not have to be like this! I remember the clean streets of our homes. I know you remember it too. There is another—"

This time she was struck in the face by a projectile. The screen paused mid-strike. Her eyes were closed, and her lips were pulled to the side.

"This doesn't help us find Jaxx." Roderic frowned. "Go back to the most recent event. Where and when is that?"

Justina appeared to be an irate woman. He could hardly blame her, but her vocalness against the Federation and their conditions would not go over well with General Sten. It was a sure way to meet an unfortunate end in Shelter City.

"That is at her home shortly before you arrived here." Yevgen's body made a slight whirring noise as he moved his head back and forth.

"This is after she brought you to the forest," Roderic said to Fiora.

She nodded that she heard him, but her hands pressed tight to her head, and she didn't speak.

When the recording reappeared, Roderic asked, "Who is she yelling at? The street looks empty."

"I believe Justina is screaming at the drones sent to do the heat counts. Though that is quite foolish," Yevgen said. "The census is happening in her sector today. Interfering with the count is punishable."

"That must have been why she was in such a hurry to get back." Roderic stared at Justina's face. "Let me see the moments before this."

"How do you get all this footage?" Fiora asked.

"That information is not up for trade." Yevgen studied Fiora's face for a moment, his eyes appearing to focus on the blood under her nose as if registering her physiological changes. "Too bad you are not a machine, for then my human computer would teach you all my secrets."

Suddenly, Yevgen's sling rolled away from them, and he disappeared behind the monitor wall.

Fiora leaned toward Roderic. "If the Federation is doing a heat count, and Jaxx is still there, we—"

Fiora flinched as Yevgen zipped toward her on the sling. Roderic automatically reached to block him and growled in warning, but the cyborg managed to spin and reach past him toward Fiora.

Yevgen touched something to the side of her head. Fiora slumped, but Roderic caught her before she fell.

"Sacred cats, Yevgen!" Roderic yelled.

"That will shut off the visions." Yevgen didn't appear concerned as he lifted a handheld medic to show Roderic. "You can place her on the cot. She should not go out into the city with those visions. It draws too much attention, attention she brings back to my home, and I do not need that."

The screens showed the people in the marketplace watching as Roderic carried Fiora through the alleyway before ending on the woman with the red scarf.

"You should have asked her before medicating her." Roderic lifted Fiora into his arms.

"Why? She would have said no." Yevgen placed his hands on the console in front of the monitors. "Her love for her husband is too strong. I made the only logical decision."

Roderic carried her to the low cot Yevgen kept in the back room and laid her down. Her nose had stopped bleeding, and the furrow had left her brow. She breathed calmly.

"I know your cyborg logic dictated you do that, but next time ask the lady." Roderic didn't like Yevgen taking the choice from Fiora but had to agree it was probably best she didn't suffer through the visions. He could see the pain they caused, which only compounded the worry she carried for her husband.

"You were telling me about Attor," Yevgen prompted.

"Jaxx first." Roderic pointed at the screen. "Show me Justina before the screaming."

The monitors blipped as Yevgen searched the area near Justina's home. The district was unremarkable as it looked like every other sector in Shelter City, only with empty streets due to the census. Yevgen tracked Justina on a center monitor as she ran from a neighbor's home to hers. She ducked inside only to return to stand in the doorway.

"What is she looking at?" Roderic leaned closer to the monitors.

The monitor showed the drones heading into her neighbor's house. The drones came for her. Lights flashed in warning. Though others looked out of their homes, no one went to help her. Justina screamed, waving her arms to draw attention to herself. "There is no need to steal my living heat. You, my jealous metal discs, may dine with us. I—"

Roderic's protective urges tried to surface as one of the drones shot a blast and hit her in the stomach. His breath caught, and his muscles tighten as if he'd been the one struck. The drones apprehended her, jerking her body at painfully odd angles as they lifted her from the ground.

Justina screamed.

His hand tightened into a fist.

"Please release me," Yevgen said. "That limb is human and can register pain, and whereas I do enjoy the occasional nerve stimulation, you are not my choice in partner."

Roderic instantly unclenched his hand. He'd been so focused on the screens he hadn't realized he'd gripped the cyborg's shoulder.

Yevgen's monitors began to flicker again, searching. "I don't have a recording of the flight, but she was taken into the facility on top of the cliff. I hope she survives her punishment. It is illegal to tamper with the heat counts."

A still image of Justina filled the screen before being filed into a grouping of photographs entitled "Federation Prisoners."

"We can't leave her..." Roderic closed his eyes and took a deep breath but found it difficult to focus. "The neighbor. She was trying to protect her neighbor. Why?"

"I'm unsure. If he was not home, he would have missed his count," Yevgen suggested.

Roderic looked at the console but had no idea how to run the equipment. "Who lives there?"

Yevgen's eyes flashed with a soft light a few times. "I've registered that it belongs to a man they call Starrs. No family."

"Show me the last time Starrs went into his house," Roderic's hands shook. He couldn't keep his mind from Justina being trapped as a prisoner. The image showed Starrs leading Justina into the home moments before she ran back out and then distracted the drones.

"Justina wasn't worried because her neighbor was missing. Starrs was there when the drones came. Maybe it was because he wasn't alone." Roderic pointed at Starrs' house. "Did you see anyone else go in before this?"

Yevgen's screens flashed. "No. I do not have that information."

"Show me where this is," Roderic insisted.

Yevgen brought up an aerial view of the city. A line appeared, showing Roderic the route to Justina's district. He quickly memorized the path.

"Don't get caught in that district when the drones come back," the cyborg warned. "They'll send your biosignature back to the Federation."

"If she wakes, don't let her leave," Roderic ordered, motioning toward Fiora. "I don't want two friends lost in the city."

"Does anyone from your generation wish to have half mates like King Attor?" Yevgen asked.

"I don't have time to tell you about that now. Just keep Justina safe," Roderic said.

Yevgen smiled. "Don't you mean Fiora?"

"Yes, that's what I said. Keep Fiora safe." Roderic started to leave.

"Wait," Yevgen ordered. Roderic rushed out the door only to hear Yevgen yell after him, "Take the handheld medic!"

Roderic went back to snatch the device from Yevgen.

"If she can't feel him, there might not be anything left to feel. Don't waste my injections on—"

Roderic left before Yevgen finished his statement. He refused to believe Jaxx was dead.

4

JUSTINA LAY ON THE PRISON CELL'S SPOTLESS white floor, unable to move from where the drones had dropped her. Bright lights shone from above, hurting her eyes. Even if she could crawl, there was no escaping them into shadows. The cell was empty.

Her cheek pressed into the cool, hard surface, contrasting the warm tear that trickled across her nose. She'd been facing down during the flight, and that was how they deposited her into the cell. Her shoulders ached. No, it was more than that. They burned as if they'd been set on fire. Moving her arms worsened the pain. She shifted her legs and her bruised knees knocked against the floor before she gave up the effort to adjust her strewn limbs.

Somehow, she'd always known she'd meet her

end like this—at the hands of the Federation. She'd been at their mercy most of her life. No one would care, and hardly anyone would notice when she didn't come home.

Except for Starrs. He would notice. He would mourn her. To everyone else, she would become a cautionary tale of what it meant not to conform.

How small her life seemed in this moment. She always thought she would have a useful life, each action a small ripple in the universes. What did that amount to now? Sure, she carried packages for her elderly neighbor, but she did not help her out of the city.

Justina closed her eyes to the lights and thought of the forest. She thought of the plants beneath her feet and the shade of tall trees over her head. And then she thought of him. Feral prince.

She played their brief encounter over in her head. Flippant words had masked her shock over seeing him shift from wild beast to naked man. Those few seconds before her feet darted to carry her home had been one of those pivotal moments, a decision that could have changed everything.

What if she'd stayed? What would have happened?

What if she said yes to his offer to leave Qurilixen?

What if she went with him? Deeper into the forest. To his palace, a place no one from Shelter City was allowed to go. Back to the stars. Into the eternal black.

Her mind conjured his image from the darkness of her thoughts. Women in the city whispered about the shifters in awe and excitement tinged with fear, but only with other women or the men who preferred men. The fantasies of being swooped up by a dragon and flown away or alone in the forest cornered by a wild cat were extremely popular.

Men in the city typically had a very different fantasy when it came to shifters. At first, when everything was new, they wanted to befriend them. Then something happened. Reality took root, and their dreams of their saviors darkened into nightmares. The change in temperament did not happen quickly, but like the drips of water off a swollen canvas. Disturbing rhetoric began filtering into the conversations—shifters as enemies, then shifters as food like any animal, then shifter blood as a cure to the lingering effects of the virus, the key to getting them back to the technology they were denied.

Violence hung palpably over all of them. Each

breath dragged it into their lungs until small pockets erupted into fights to ease collective anger. Those fights were ragged bandages. Soon they would tear and be useless to stop the inevitable darkness.

Darkness.

The idea lingered in her mind. She thought of what her father once told her when she asked what death was like for her mother. He said the end was simply closing one's eyes and swirling into darkness, a dreamless dream devoid of pain.

Would the darkness come for her now?

Justina frowned and peeked through her lids into the bright light. Maybe that's why the one night of darkness that came to the planet each year terrified her. What a horrible idea to give a frightened child.

The naked image of the prince in the forest again came to mind, the thought scaring away the darkness. The other women would be jealous of what she'd seen, such virile strength and determined eyes. Feral. The word fit him well.

What if she'd gone with him? To the palace. To his home. To his bed. To touch that shifting skin. To feel something, anything, that wasn't pain.

What would it have been like to be born into his world? They shared a planet, but their experiences were very different. What would it be like to not have to worry about the next meal? To come and go as she pleased? To marry and love and have a family? To change who she was and run wild in the forest, so fierce everyone she came across would fear her claws?

There was danger in daydreams, in hope. The Cysgodians had learned that the hardest of ways.

Justina drew her bruised knees toward her waist, prepared for the pain it caused. She screamed, a half growl, half shriek as she forced her body to twist and push upright. Her arms hung limp as she knelt on the floor. The sound of her heavy breathing filled the silence.

"Hey-oh!" Justina yelled. "You can't leave me in here. I need a medic."

No one answered, but she had a feeling a guard watched.

"Your drones did this to my arms. You owe me a medic." She kept her words forceful, but they contradicted the tears building in her eyes. "I can't work without my arms. Don't you want me to work?"

That was assuming they would let her go.

5

THE ANIMAL INSIDE RODERIC WANTED TO TEAR out of his skin and run through the streets. The locals seeing him on the ground would not be the same as dragons patrolling the air, and such a thing would be considered a violation of the Federation agreement.

Maybe their elders were right. Perhaps they should just stay out of the city.

Even as he thought it, even as he made his way through the streets looking for his missing friend, he knew they couldn't ignore the plight of so many.

In the fear he tried to suppress, memories surfaced. He couldn't remember a time when he hadn't known Jaxx. It was impossible to count the nights spent camping in the woods, hunting in the

Northern Mountains in Draig territory, climbing the rock formations south of the Var palace, sneaking away from a banquet to drink and cause mischief. Or in the last decades, planning and plotting how they were going to smuggle food and medical care into Shelter City.

Roderic tucked the handheld medic under his arm, cradling the device against his chest. He kept his head down, glancing up to navigate the crowds as he hurried through the city. His senses prickled as he tracked his surroundings. Feet shuffled over dirt. Someone struck a piece of canvas. The loud *thud-thud-thud* sounded like a series of punches.

"...took the madwoman always yelling..." a woman's voice disappeared into the crowd.

Roderic slowed his steps and listened for the conversation.

"Who?" a man asked.

"Justina, everyone knows Justina." The woman sighed. "You threw mud at her."

"Census violation? So they finally got her for something. That's too bad."

Roderic found the man who spoke. He was blocked by the busy street, but his dark hair stood out like a ratted mess in the crowd.

"Too bad? Why's that?" the woman with him asked.

"She made an easy target."

The couple laughed. Roderic's fist tightened.

An older woman stomped toward them and swatted the man on the shoulder.

"Ow, Shirl, what?" the man protested.

"You shouldn't mock others' misfortunes, or you might call them onto yourself." Shirl smacked him a second time and then motioned for him to walk. "No one deserves to see the inside of those prisons. Justina's a good girl. She fetched my rations for me when I was too sick to go."

Roderic quickened his pace. First Jaxx. Then he'd figure out what to do about Justina.

"But it's not my fault, he—" a young boy tried to protest as he passed in front of Roderic.

An older woman gripped the boy's arm, dragging him down the street in a great show of upset. "If you go around looking for a reason to be offended, you will find it. Now get home."

The soft, unmistakable grunt of faulty technology caught his attention seconds before he smelled rotting meat. He bowed his head to avoid eye contact with the two Sweeper borgs walking in his direction. The units were reconditioned rubbish collecting droids that the Federation used as brutes to police the citizens of Shelter City. Though the borgs had several parts that appeared humanoid, their electronic eyes gave them away as they focused on their surroundings.

Roderic couldn't afford the attention, so he ducked to the side and pretended to look at baskets woven from bark. The woman selling them didn't bother to stand. Her tired eyes stared at the ground as if wishing it would open up and take her to a new reality. If he carried anything of value, he would have traded with the woman but he had not been prepared for this trip into the city.

Roderic waited until the Sweeper borgs passed before moving on. As he walked into Justina's district, the streets became eerily quiet. Several people stared at him from their doorways as if too afraid to move even though there were no drones above. A few closed their doors as if refusing him entry before he tried.

His heartbeat quickened as he caught sight of Justina's house. Marks disrupted the dirt where her feet had stumbled before the drones flew her away. He looked at the green-tinted sky, but it was empty except for the three suns.

Roderic went to Starr's door and struck the palm

of his hand against it several times. "Open up. I need to talk to you!"

No one answered.

Roderic leaned his ear against the door. Inside was still.

He glanced down the empty street before pushing his way into the home. His eyes shifted to see in the dim light. Someone had stacked junk and spare parts into neat piles. Beyond the rusted metal and dirt, he detected the smell of blood. He followed the scent to a large mound of wood.

He discovered a darker patch on the dirt floor and lightly touched it with the tips of his fingers. Mud clung to them as he lifted them to his nose. No doubt, this was blood, and it wasn't human.

"Jaxx?" Roderic called, listening as he quickly scanned every dark corner. The house appeared to be empty.

He hurried outside and took a deep breath. Now that he knew what he looked for, he picked up the scent of shifter blood. He ran through Justina's open door. Her smell filled his deep breath. The floor had been swept clean. A mat with a patched blanket laid on the floor in the middle of the room. A stack of rolled parchments was neatly arranged in a corner next to an old reader with a cracked screen. Under her scent came a trace of stale bread. He looked up to see a food bag hanging high from the ceiling.

As many times as he'd walked through Shelter City, he'd never gone into the homes. Justina had joked about not having furniture, but he never thought it might be true.

He hated the Federation for allowing General Sten leadership over this post. No man with honor would stand for this poverty.

Perhaps it was time they broke the agreement. The standoff between the shifters and the Federation was going nowhere, and the Cysgodians were suffering because of it.

He wanted to protect his people and his planet.

He wanted to help the alien visitors.

He wanted the Federation gone.

Nothing could be done right now because he needed to find Jaxx.

Roderic shut Justina's door as he left and tracked the scent of blood between Starrs and Justina's homes. Like the entrance to Yevgen's house, the narrow opening could hardly be considered a walkway, yet drag marks led to the closed end.

Roderic turned to the side and followed the tracks. The smell of blood became more substantial, and he detected a soft *swish-swish* from the other side of the metal wall. He braced his foot on Justina's home and used it as leverage to jump onto her roof.

The sound of Roderic's landing startled Starrs. The man stood over a hole in the hidden yard behind the homes. His eyes rounded in shock as he lifted his hands and moved to hide the opening from view but not before Roderic saw two Draig-style boots poking out.

He leaped down and instantly charged the man. The handheld medic slipped from his grasp. Starrs jumped out of his way. Roderic squared off against the man, ready for a fight.

Starrs lifted his hands to indicate he meant no harm and pointed at the hole. "Help."

The feet didn't move as Roderic leaned over to peer into the hole. Jaxx had been crammed inside the narrow space, and there was no easy way to lift him out. He tried to detect whether or not his friend breathed, but the smell of dirt and blood clouded his senses.

"What happened?" Roderic demanded. He began pulling on Jaxx's feet.

Starrs joined him and began pushing to counteract Roderic's efforts. "Help."

Roderic grabbed Starrs' arm to stop him.

"Help." Starrs pointed to the sky. "Him."

"You're hiding him from the drones?"

Starrs nodded.

"Help me get him out of this hole," Roderic ordered, grabbing both legs as he tried to extricate his friend. He braced his feet and leaned as he pulled.

Starrs hesitated.

Roderic let his eyes shift in warning, knowing the inner glow would frighten the man. "Before the drones come back and catch us."

Starrs nodded and kneeled by the hole. He reached for one of Jaxx's thighs.

Jaxx's body finally let loose, and he slid from the hole onto the ground. Roderic hurried to check on him. His stomach was wrapped with a strip of material that matched the dress Justina wore in the woods, but blood was seeping from the wound. A lump had formed on his head, and though his chest lifted, the breaths were raspy and shallow.

Roderic placed a hand on his chest and breathed a sigh of relief. "He's alive. Barely."

"Help," Starrs said, the words stunted and short. "Hurry."

"Get me the handheld." Roderic pointed to the device he'd dropped on the ground.

Starrs shuffled toward the medic and picked it up. Curious, he examined it, turning the device in his hands as he brought it back.

A claw extended from the tip of Roderic's finger, and he slashed at the bandage to cut it free before ripping through Jaxx's shirt to expose his stomach. Blood oozed from a stab wound. Roderic snatched the handheld medic from Starrs and programmed the device to clean and seal the injury.

Usually, shifters could heal themselves, at least enough to avoid this amount of blood loss. Var scientists taught that it had to do with the way their cells mutated and expanded during the change. The fact Jaxx's body wasn't self-healing meant something much more serious was wrong.

"He needs a medical booth," Roderic said, more to himself. Handhelds worked for emergencies, but they weren't as good as a full scan. The nearest booth he could use would be at the Var palace.

"No." Starrs rubbed the side of his head. "Booth."

"I know." Roderic moved the device along the wound, ignoring the smell of lasered flesh. "You're not given access to medical booths."

When the wound no longer bled, Roderic pressed the device to Jaxx's forehead. It flashed several times as it scanned Jaxx's brain. The stats that came onto the screen weren't good, but at least they were stabilizing.

"The drones took Justina." Roderic tried not to think about the drones flying off with the woman or what the Federation guards might be doing to her. He glanced at Starrs. "You're friends with her? She was protecting you?"

Starrs nodded and looked up at the sky. "Help."

The device vibrated in his hand. Roderic wasn't a doctor, so he put the medic to walk him through the functions. It prompted him to place the injector next to Jaxx's neck.

"What will happen to her for interrupting the census?" he asked.

A tear slid down Starrs' cheek when he lowered his head. His worried expression answered for him.

"She helped my friends at a great risk to herself." Roderic moved the unit and rested it against Jaxx's chest. The dragon prince's breath deepened, and color returned to his features. "I promise, I'll do everything I can to make sure she's released."

The man did not appear comforted by his words. Roderic couldn't blame him. He had no reason to trust outsiders.

And yet, he had helped Jaxx at significant risk to himself.

"And we are also in your debt," Roderic said.

"He." Starrs gestured at Jaxx.

"He'll live. Thank you for protecting him."

"He," Starrs repeated, seeming to have difficulty forming his words. "Kind."

"Yes." Roderic nodded.

"To me," Starrs finished. He pulled a cover over the hole to hide it.

Roderic moved the handheld back to Jaxx's neck. He focused his shifter hearing and detected a slight buzz in the distance. "I'll get him out of your district as soon as he's awake enough to drag out of here. You should go back into your home for the heat counts. I think the drones are back in the air."

Starrs placed a hand on Roderic's shoulder as he passed. His eyes moved to the handheld device but didn't linger. He pulled back a piece of metal sheeting and ducked out of sight behind it.

"Jaxx, time to wake up," Roderic ordered, his voice stern. "I'll carry you if I have to, but it'll draw attention."

The sound of the drones became increasingly louder. The entire weight of the situation came down on him. This was more than protecting Jaxx or helping Justina. They were two princes from the two royal shifter families. They couldn't be caught in the city. Their presence would break the agreement, and the Federation would claim permanent residence.

Shifters called Shelter City a temporary settlement because to do anything else would be to acknowledge a territory that the Federation had dominion over. General Sten would claim the Federation had control over the land and would absorb Qurilixen into the Federation's Planetary Alliance. And that would be the end of their way of life.

The handheld finished its injections. Roderic pulled it away from Jaxx's neck. "Get up, old friend. Fiora needs you."

Jaxx's eyes opened. "Fiora?"

"She's safe. She's with Yevgen. I'll take you to her." Roderic pushed Jaxx's shoulder to sit him upright. "Can you walk?"

Jaxx tried to nod, even as he swayed. Pain tinted his words. "Flying would be easier."

"You can't. You'll be seen." Roderic hoisted him to his feet. He half-walked, half-dragged him to the metal sheeting. "Census drones are coming to do a heat count. We can't be here."

Jaxx wobbled and lost his footing as he looked toward the sky. Roderic caught him but dropped the handheld.

"I hear them," Jaxx said, his voice faint.

Roderic pulled the metal aside and urged Jaxx through. He swiped the handheld from the ground before following him. Taking Jaxx's arm, he forced him to walk faster between the houses. When they emerged, he slid his arm behind his back to support his weight as he quickened their pace.

"What are you doing here? I thought you were camping in the forest," Jaxx asked, stumbling and dragging his feet. His eyes started to drift closed as if he might pass out again.

Roderic flexed his arm to support more of Jaxx's weight. "A local woman named Justina brought Fiora to me in the woods. Fiora's visions were overloading her, and she made little sense. She refused to stay behind when I came to look for you, so I brought her to Yevgen. He drugged her. She's sleeping. I promise, she's safe."

Jaxx walked with him for several steps as they maneuvered out of the empty streets into the crowds. Roderic evened their pace so Jaxx could keep up easier.

"What is it? I can sense something is wrong."

Jaxx leaned against a wooden post and took several deep breaths. His eyes again closed, and Roderic decided it might be best to keep him talking.

"Drones took Justina. I don't know what they will do to her. She sacrificed herself to save your life." Roderic glanced up at the sky. The drones were moving back into Justina's district. "And Fiora's."

"Then we'll go after her," Jaxx responded, as if such a conclusion was the only answer. "But there's more. We've known each other too long, and I know that look in your eyes. What are you not telling me? Did my wife say something about the future?"

Roderic thought about lying. Standing in a crowded street was no place to have this conversation. Slowly, he nodded. "She said I was in for heartache and pain, then pointed at the sky."

"And drones flew Justina overhead when she said it?" Jaxx concluded.

"The sky was empty. I don't know what Fiora meant by it," Roderic answered.

Jaxx stood quiet for a few moments longer before motioning Roderic to walk.

"Sky? That could mean several things. Fiora's visions in crowded places are a jumbled mess or they *were* before we were married."

"This thing," Roderic gestured with the handheld, "indicated you hit your head. Maybe your unconscious state kept you from easing the burden of her visions, which caused them to flood back."

"Perhaps."

"What happened to you? Were you attacked?" Roderic quizzed his friend.

"I'm embarrassed to say," Jaxx grumbled. "Some men jumped me in an alley and rifled through my pockets. I didn't sense them coming until they had a knife in my gut. I was... distracted."

"Distracted by...?"

Jaxx gave a weak laugh. "My wife's ass."

Roderic suppressed the urge to laugh. "You were overtaken because you were staring at your wife's backside? You're lucky you survived, or else I would feel bad when I tell everyone about this."

Jaxx grinned. "You can't, or you admit we were in the city."

"That's a stupid rule." Roderic sighed. "I might modify the details, but I'm still telling it."

"Do you think the sky premonition meant alien visitor? I hear the Syog are returning to the planet soon," Jaxx mused in an obvious attempt to make Roderic laugh. "Their women are aggressive. I'll be happy to act as your forward in presenting an offer to their most, um, *assertive* females."

Roderic automatically flinched and resisted the urge to cover his manhood. The Syog had interesting ways of settling disputes, none of which boded well for the males. "I'd rather break the war treaty and marry your cousin."

"Grace is a dragon. That could be what the sky vision is about. I love her, but she would mean heartache for any man." Jaxx chuckled. "With her temper, she'd probably set your manhood on fire at least once a fortnight. Though I would say her anger toward relationships is justified. It can't be easy being forced to marry. For her or for Prince Korbin. Political maneuverings don't guarantee strong mates."

Since before they were born, Korbin and Grace had been betrothed as part of a peace treaty between dragons and cats to end a centuries-long war. The parents had thought it to be a symbolic gesture that would fade over time. Unfortunately, their people took it seriously, and many wanted the wedding to happen. Since it hadn't, if either royal was seen showing an interest in another person, whispers of treason would erupt throughout the shifters. So,

Grace and Korbin avoided each other like carriers of the blue plague.

"Korbin has been talking about space travel again," Roderic said.

"Can't say I blame him. Eyes watch him closer than most." Jaxx pressed the back of his hand to his mouth and coughed.

"Maybe I should run away with him." Roderic frowned as Jaxx coughed harder. "That cough sounds bad. You need a medical booth."

When Jaxx pulled his hand away, blood dotted his fingers. "I need to see my wife."

They made their way through the city, back to the narrow entrance of Yevgen's home. Roderic had Jaxx go in first as he watched the streets. When no one looked, he slipped in behind him.

"There was something off about the men who came for me," Jaxx whispered as he sidestepped his way toward the door. He braced his hand against the metal wall with each step.

"How so?" Roderic observed Jaxx's movements, ready to catch his friend if he fell over.

"Their eyes. Maybe their smell?" Jaxx shook his head. "I don't know what it was. They weren't...right."

"Did they know you were a dragon? Were they

after your blood?" Roderic thought of the stories he'd heard of Cysgodians wanting to consume shifters for their power.

"I don't think so. At least, not at first," Jaxx paused, touching his side. "Maybe it was the shock of the attack. But their eyes weren't right. They were..."

"Let's get you inside." Roderic nudged him gently to keep walking. "You can rest by your wife, and I'll have Yevgen check you with this handheld. He'll know its programming better than I do."

"What will you do?"

"I have to find Justina. She saved you. We owe her." Even as Roderic said the words, he knew there was more to his desire to help the woman than the repayment of kindness. The sound of her voice echoed through his mind.

"You don't find me. Ever. This is the end of our story, prince. We're written in two very different books."

He couldn't accept that.

"I can't leave her..." Roderic heard the sound of Yevgen's door shutting. Jaxx had already gone inside.

6

Justina's voice had become hoarse from yelling into the empty space. She sat on the hard floor, staring at the outline of a handleless door, willing it to open. No matter how hard she begged and threatened, no one answered her.

The room had been sterilized, and she noticed the contrast between the floor and her dirty, ripped clothes. The jagged tear reminded her of the bleeding shifter Starrs had dragged home. She hoped he'd listened to her and shoved the man down into the hole before the drones returned for the count. Otherwise, the pain she was in now would all be for nothing.

She found a smudge of dirt on her dress and wished she could move her arms to scratch at it. The pattern somewhat resembled the cat-shifter, and the color matched the soil in the tunnel. Her thoughts turned back to the forest, then to the man standing naked in the trees.

"You don't look like a prince," she whispered to the stain.

"What do princes look like?"

"Less feral," she answered the memory, saying the exact words she had before. She kept her voice soft as if doing so would keep her from being over-heard. "I imagine most princes would wear clothing."

"Does my nakedness alarm you?"

She had laughed at the question, but now she answered honestly. "Yes."

Justina closed her eyes, wondering what it would have felt like to walk toward him, to touch warm skin and hard muscles. What would his breath feel like whispering across her cheek?

"Does my nakedness affect you?"

"Yes."

"Does my nakedness attract you?"

"Yes."

The available men in Shelter City didn't interest her. Marriages weren't like what they were on their old planet. Her parents had loved each other. Starrs loved his wife. Those relationships seemed like a luxury they couldn't afford. Now marriages were based more on living arrangements and food rations.

But the prince in the forest wasn't from Shelter City. He wouldn't be like the other men she met.

"I'm not supposed to be here," she whispered to the cat-shaped stain. "None of us are."

"Wait," she remembered him saying as he tried to stop her from leaving. *"How can I find you?"*

"You don't find me, prince." Justina smiled, no longer seeing the room as her vision blurred. "This is the end of our story. We're written in two very different books."

"Come with me to my palace."

In reality, she had said no, but now she whispered, "Yes. I will go with you."

"Come with me."

"Yes." A tear slid down her cheek onto the stain. She watched the moisture spread into a dark spot along the image of the cat's stomach.

"Come with—"

"No. I can't." Reality trickled its way in. Even in a fantasy, she couldn't leave Starrs behind or risk upsetting the balance between the Federation and the locals who'd given them sanctuary.

"First time?"

Justina looked up at the man's voice. His black uniform contrasted with the white room. She hadn't heard the Federation guard enter the room. The doorway had slid open, and she could see behind him into a hall. Instinct tried to push her to her feet. Physical limitations kept her on the ground.

He lifted an electronic clipboard and tapped on the screen. "While we appreciate your enthusiasm, next time it's not necessary to be so convincing. A little blood will do."

Justina stared at the man, not knowing what he meant. The word *Sever* appeared on his uniform.

"They explained to you how this works, right?" He dropped the clipboard to his side and signed heavily. "You get into a little trouble—a *little*, no need to dislocate both your arms unless you're into that kind of thing. You'll be brought here, held for a short time, given medical care, your special food rations, and then returned to the city to deposit your product. Your record will have a mark on it, but it will fade in time. If you get into trouble with your people, that's your risk. We'll handle our end."

Justina continued to stare.

"Can you speak?" His words became clipped.

Justina nodded. The pain in her arms radiated throughout her body, and she imagined the only thing keeping her upright was his condescending stare. He started to lean closer but then wrinkled his nose and quickly withdrew.

"You're quiet. General Sten likes the quiet ones." Sever tilted his head back and forth to look at her. "We could clean you up, put you in a nice dress and present you to the general."

Justina's eyes widened, and she shook her head in denial.

"All his mistresses are fed well." Sever glanced down and lifted up the clipboard as if he couldn't quite deliver the sales pitch. "And bathed."

Justina again shook her head. She'd rather be kept in this cell with her useless arms.

"Distribution, then. On your back." He tapped his clipboard.

Justina didn't move. For one, it hurt too badly. But mostly, she would never get on her back for a Federation soldier.

"You're all wild creatures," he muttered. "It's like they killed the intelligent ones with the virus."

Justina wondered if she spun her body, would her arm flop enough to slap him?

Sever pointed at the ceiling, to where panels slid open. "Medical lasers will fix you. On your back."

The floor beneath her shifted and moved,

pushing her from the ground as it turned into a medical table. Lasers activated from above, their green lights dancing over her as she slowly maneuvered onto her back. Warmth spread over her as the lasers worked.

Sever monitored the scan on his clipboard. "Two dislocated shoulders. Kidney mass. Lung mass. Malnutrition—*though that's not surprising.* Scar tissue inner thigh. Head trauma. Broken finger. Brain swelling. Bone mass."

Justina laid tense, trying not to move as the lasers traveled over her. She watched as they concentrated their light on various parts of her body.

"Keep breathing, or you'll give the wrong readings," Sever ordered. "You're not in the best of health, are you?" He again sighed as if the sound was meant to scold her. "We don't have time for everything. We'll fix the main issues."

Justina felt heat against her neck as the above lasers changed color and moved their beams to her shoulders. The sensation prickled. Suction pulled at her from behind, and both shoulders made loud popping noises. She gasped in surprise but breathed a sigh of relief as the pain lessened. Just as her body began to relax, a clamp shot from below and locked her head against the table. She cried out in fright at the sudden attack.

Sever laughed. "So you do have a voice."

Justina clawed at her head, pushing against the clamp to try to slide out. A second clamp wound round her neck, holding her in place. She kicked her legs violently.

"There is life in there after all." Sever stood over her.

She reached for him, trying to grab hold.

He laughed harder and jumped back. "Easy, or it'll cook your brains."

Justina swiped at him one last time before grabbing the vice around her neck and pulling as hard as she could manage. She braced her feet on the table for leverage. It did no good.

"Hold still." Sever firmly pushed down her knee, and a restraint clamped her ankle. "Ugh—*there*." Her second leg was more of a struggle, but she couldn't fight his weight as he leaned over her. "Are you sure you wouldn't like to meet the general instead? He likes taming the wild ones."

"I thought you said he likes them," Justina inhaled a shaky breath as the lasers hit her forehead only to weakly finish, "quiet."

The pain in her head eased, and her thoughts

cleared. However, fear grew to settle in her chest. A sharp, burning poke in her ass told her she'd been injected with something. Her muscles weakened. Sever blurred, and she blinked to keep him in focus.

"The truth is, he doesn't care. You all break in the end," he said.

She opened her mouth, but only a weak moan came out. Her lids fell heavy over her eyes, and she closed them for a short moment to gather her strength.

"Get up. Time to go."

Justina felt another sting against her ass cheek. The table moved beneath her, and she opened her eyes. Her head and legs were free, and she quickly sat up even as the table turned into the floor. Sever stood, arms crossed, watching as she lowered.

When she sat on the ground once more, he uncrossed his arms to hold out his hand to show her a small vial. "Be careful with this."

Justina slowly took it from him. It was warm from his body heat. She wanted to ask what it was, but his actions seemed to indicate that he would free her because of whatever he thought she was doing there. She determined it best to stay quiet for fear she'd give her ignorance away.

"One drop into the food of your target and then

get out of the area. Any more than that, and it'll be too obvious." Sever motioned for her to stand. "You should know the medical scan found several abnormal growths. You haven't been using food simulators or decontaminators, have you? There is a reason we keep them out of the city. We have some of the best scientists, and they warned you that exposure to even the most minuscule radiation from the units will make your people sick."

Justina shook her head.

"The growths won't kill you right away, but..."

He let the words hang like a death sentence.

"Can you..." She pushed to her feet and watched his face for any sign of compassion. There was none. "...fix them?

"I can." Sever nodded. "But I find people work harder when there is an incentive to do so. You distribute that whole vial and come back for a refill. We'll take care of one of the masses for you. And, in case you lose your nerve or happen to get caught, remember, I'm your access to a medical booth, and it will be in your interest to stay quiet."

"Who...?" She lifted the vial. The dark liquid was filled to the top. There were a lot of drops inside the small container.

"Anyone with a short temper and preferably

great strength. Around crowds are best. The more chaos, the better." Sever motioned for her to move toward the door. "Step out so I can sanitize the room."

Justina walked sideways to keep an eye on him as she inched toward the doorway. When she made it to the hall, she glanced in both directions only to find they looked exactly the same. She fought the urge to run—not that she knew where to run to if she tried.

He laughed as if reading her thoughts. "You can try."

Sever stepped out and pushed a series of buttons on the wall next to the door. Blue light flooded the white room to start the sanitation process as the door slid shut.

Justina fingered the vial. "This won't kill anyone, will it?"

"I have to recall some of the recruiters. They're not doing a particularly good job of explaining before sending you up here. Who did you talk to?" Sever started walking, prompting her to follow.

Justina kept her mouth shut.

"All you need to know is that what you hold in your hand is your ticket to more food rations. With the new shortages coming, I'm sure you can admit it's a small thing to do. Now, do you think you can handle this? Or do we need to explore other options for you?"

Justina knew she could only give one answer. She nodded. "I can do it."

"Good. This is one key to a very complicated puzzle you can't possibly understand. In fact, you don't need to understand." Sever turned a corner and placed his hand against a door scanner. "Wait here."

He disappeared inside, leaving her alone. They apparently weren't too worried about her running off. She looked at the vial as it rolled in her palm. When she returned home, she would...what? Throw it away? Dump it out? Risk being brought back here because she didn't do what they asked?

Sever returned with a small bundle. He placed it on her outstretched hand on top of the vial. "Hide it or eat it before you get to the city. Or dose the food and hand it out. Remember, we're always watching."

He strode ahead of her, taking several more turns.

They passed a couple of guards who eyed her with bored curiosity before continuing their conversation. Their laughter followed behind her, and she thought she heard something about her dress. She tucked her arms across her chest, feeling very small.

Soon the bright green-tinted light from outside shone through a large opening at the end of the complex, and the scent of fresh air replaced that of the sterile facility. She took a deep breath. Trees appeared in the distance.

"Take the path down to the city. Tell them you received medical treatment at the benevolence of the general." Sever paused as he waved back the two guards at the entrance. He lowered his voice. "If any guards scan you, they'll see a report filed. The faster you get through your drops, the sooner you can get that mass off your kidney. Otherwise, you're going to urinate blood in a few months. When you're ready, get into a little trouble, and the drones will bring you back up."

Before she could say anything, he turned away from her and strode into the facility. She stared after him.

"What just happened?" Justina whispered to herself. She saw the two guards eyeing her, and she quickly moved toward the path that would take her to the city before they could stop her. By all right, she should be imprisoned right now. She hung the food from her belt and looped the edge of her skirt over it to hide the bundle. Dresses were a nuisance, but General Sten preferred them on females. Back when they did clothing rations, that was what they'd been given to wear.

Air hit the side of her bared leg, but she didn't care. As soon as she got home, she'd share the food with Starrs and together they'd figure out what to do about the vial.

7

RODERIC DIDN'T KNOW WHAT HIS PLAN WAS exactly, but he was going to find a way into that black hole of a facility, and he wasn't leaving until he had Justina with him. His father was a dignitary, after all, and it was a position Roderic had been born to take over someday. It wouldn't be strange if Prince Roderic of the Var requested a tour of the facility, would it?

This was a weak plan and a bad idea.

Still, it was better than storming the halls with claws extended, fighting his way like a wild animal until he found her. The cat inside him voted for that plan, fueled by decades of frustration over the treatment of Shelter City.

No, not a wild animal. Feral. She'd called him feral. Feral prince.

The idea of Justina being trapped in the facility caused anger to bubble up inside him. He told himself it was because she'd saved his friends. The animal inside him laughed at that excuse. His more primal nature knew something the man in him clearly did not want to admit. Justina stirred him— her voice, her stare, her honor.

"You should know better than to offer an escape. If General Sten catches us breaking the deal between the Federation and shifters, he'll retaliate in a way that would be bad for both our people."

He'd offered her a clear path to freedom, and she hadn't even stopped selfishly to consider the option. All it took was those brief seconds, and he felt he already knew *almost* all he needed to about her. She was worthy of their protection. Surely none of the shifter elders would disagree with his actions when he explained what she'd done for Jaxx and Fiora.

Yeah, logic wasn't buying that either. They would understand his motivation, but they wouldn't condone his actions. Too much was at stake.

He thought of Jaxx collapsed next to his wife on the cot in Yevgen's home. The couple would live, and they were together. Thanks to Justina and Starrs.

He thought of the Federation gaining a stronger foothold on Qurilixen. When they took Fiora prisoner, the Federation brought her from outer space. So when the shifters saved her, the Draig queen—who by some miracle had memorized the minutiae of the agreement—was able to use it against the Federation. They had to declare any off-world prisoners brought to the facility. Since they had not, Fiora was free to be with Jaxx. If the Federation broke the agreement, the shifters could eject them from the planet.

Justina was different. She was a Cysgodian. They had control over her fate, which included keeping her prisoner for breaking their city's laws. If they caught him trying to break the agreement by freeing her, the Federation could use that as an excuse to claim squatter rights to the territory and never leave. They'd spread their soldiers like an infection, and the general would demand to have a say over intergalactic matters.

Roderic paused in the trees just out of sight of the entrance. If he did this...

If he didn't do this...

If he...

"Justina." Her name left his lips, breaking through his thoughts even before he realized he'd caught her scent on the breeze.

His heart hammered so loudly it echoed in his ears. He held his breath, letting his eyes shift to better take in the distance. He stared at the facility and watched as she emerged from within next to a Federation guard. She wasn't restrained.

Roderic tilted his head and used his shifter hearing to listen to what they said.

"Tell them you received medical treatment at the benevolence of the general," the soldier said. His words became muffled as he turned his head away from where Roderic hid. "...your drops...mass off your kidney... you're going to urinate blood...trouble...you back."

Kidney? Blood? Justina was ill, and they gave her something called drops?

Why not a medical booth?

Claws erupted from his hand as a shiver of warning crawled along his flesh. The cougar inside him was restless and angry. He took several deep breaths, forcing himself to calm down and watch.

Justina tucked a bundle under her belt and hid it under the edge of her torn skirt before hurrying away from the facility. They had let her go. She looked healthier than she had in the recording.

The decision to invade the facility to find her was taken from him. Thank the gods because he'd been about to incite a war for her.

Roderic watched her make her way toward the path that would lead her back into Shelter City. He stalked through the forest, stepping lightly as he passed through the trees. When he couldn't see her, he listened for her. When she reached the path that would take her down to the valley, he rushed to join her. Only a small section of the trail was hidden from both the facility's entrance and those below by a large, deformed tree growing out of the cliffside.

He looked over the edge to where she'd started walking down an incline. "Justina."

She jumped in fright and spun around before finding him above her. Seeing him, she again glanced around in panic. She moved a few steps back and whispered up to him. "What are you doing here? You can't be here."

"Give me your hand." He reached for her. "I'll pull you up."

"I can't. I have to..." She looked at the vial she held. "I have to..."

"I saw Starrs. He's safe."

"You did?" She took a couple more steps, coming closer. "Was it before or after the heat count?"

"I took Jaxx out of there before. Starrs went into his house as the drones were coming back. They're both safe." Since she wasn't taking his offered hand, he placed it on the edge of the cliff and hopped down to join her on the narrow walkway, blocking her from continuing further down the path. "Thanks to you."

"You're welcome. Now you should leave." She leaned back to glance down at the city beyond the barracks below them. "You can't be here. A guard could come up and see you."

"Then come with me." He found himself standing a little too close. He couldn't help it. Something about her eyes drew him in and mesmerized him.

"Why?"

His gaze moved to her mouth as she formed the word.

"You..." For a moment, Roderic forgot his reasons. He wanted to kiss that mouth.

"I don't have time for this," she said, finishing his thought with one of her own. With a firm push at his arm, she ordered, "Go. Now. Before you get us both into trouble."

Her touch sent a shockwave through him like a blaster set to stun. He didn't leave. "Is Starrs your man?"

"What?" She stiffened in surprise. "I, ah, that's, um... We're not talking about this. I barely know you."

"Is he? Are you taken?" Roderic tensed, suddenly needing to know the answer.

"Is that really why you stopped me? To ask me about a man?" She frowned at him. "If I tell you, will you go?"

Roderic nodded.

"Starrs is my oldest friend. Our families met on the transport ship on the way over. There is no one I care more about in all the universes. He took care of me after my father died." She pushed his arm to make him leave. "He still takes care of me. And he needs me to help take care of him."

Roderic didn't move. "So no man?"

"Yes. I have a man."

He'd rather she punched him than hear the admission.

"He's large and likes to bite off the ears of men who stand too close to me. Now go. Have a nice life, feral prince." She shoved him harder and made a move to stride past him.

Roderic lifted his arm to the side to keep her from leaving. "Come with me."

"Stop offering that." She tried to move around him the other way.

Roderic lifted his other arm to block her. "I'm honor-bound to repay you. Twice."

"If you want to repay me, don't get me in trouble now." She placed her hands on her hips, and it looked as if she contemplated pushing him off the side of the cliff or at least onto the misshapen tree. "I'm sorry, but I can't risk being seen talking to you."

"It doesn't work that way. You saved two lives. Royal lives. Shifters live by a code." Though technically accurate, he threw in the fact that Jaxx and Fiora were royals to make it sound more important. In truth, shifters saw all of their lives worth preserving and repaying—from farmer to warrior to prince to alien visitors. "We owe you. And Starrs."

"I relieve you of the debt, feral prince." She let loose a long sigh. "Both of them. Now go."

"Only the gods can relieve me of such a thing." Roderic lowered his arms and threaded his fingers together. "Give me your foot. I'll boost you up. I think I hear someone coming from below."

Justina frowned. Shaking her head, she moved up the path and then hopped up on the topside on her own. She hurried into the forest to hide from view.

Roderic leaped onto the cliff and followed her. She walked several paces away from the facility before stopping to face him. "I can't leave Shelter City."

"They did the census in your area. I can have you back before the next one. No one will know you're gone." Roderic tried to think of a more compelling reason than the ones filtering through his thoughts involving her mouth and eyes and his desire to stare at them for hours.

Justina clenched her fist. "If you want to repay me, bring food the next time you come to the city. I have it on good authority there are more food shortages coming."

That information snapped him out of his wandering thoughts. Roderic frowned. "They can't do that."

"General Sten would apparently disagree with you. He can do whatever he wants to us. No one is standing up to stop him." Justina turned to go.

"We have food simulators." Roderic offered. "I've spoken to a trusted scientist, and she doesn't believe the radiation from them will cause the harm the Federation claims. At least not compared to starvation. If you come with me, she can run tests. Don't you want your people to have answers, real answers?"

"We *have* real answers. One percent. How is that's for an answer?" Justina stretched her hands to the side as she spoke to illustrate her point. "Less than one percent of our entire planet's population survived the virus. Less than one lucky percent made it all the way here for the promised cure of the blue radiation. And it worked. This planet's atmosphere killed the virus. But for what?"

She turned in the direction of the city.

"For this." She made a weak noise as if choking back emotions. "We're alive, barely, but this isn't a life. Our life spans are not what they were. They tell us the virus did something to us. We're dying younger. We can't use your food simulators because they tell us the radiation will make us die even faster. We can't use decontaminators. Our temporary settlement was put in this valley so we'd get large doses of direct blue sunlight for most hours of the day. But what the valley doesn't have is a water source for bathing. Trust me, prince, I have about all the real answers I can handle."

Roderic inched closer to where she stood, only to stop when she turned back to face him. He waited to see if she would back away from him. She didn't.

"How do you think the Federation provides food rations for the entire city?" Roderic insisted. "They don't trade with us for grains, and they don't bring enough cargo onto the planet—*that we can see*—to supply even meager rations."

They might have brought cargo that the shifters didn't detect. General Sten did sneak people on-world without permission, usually on the one night of darkness that happened each year. Yet, Roderic doubted the man bothered hauling expensive food provisions.

"They have simulators," he told her. "I've seen them when we did a dignitary tour of the facility. Their resources are endless. They can afford to feed a hundred cities without resorting to rations."

Justina crossed her arms over her chest and stared at the ground. "Maybe the low rations are to contain radiation levels from the simulators? Maybe any more than that, and we'll get sick again."

"Do you believe that?" Roderic hated her defeated stance. Instinct told him to comfort her, but he wouldn't hold her without her permission, and she kept her arms protectively crossed.

"I don't know what to believe." A tear slipped over her cheek. "I'm just...tired. We're hungry all the time. We lost our homeworld, and this place is...dirty and I... They don't let us use the decontaminators, and if they do, it's like the only holiday we have left to celebrate. I lost my family. Starrs is... He needs me, and I'm—"

"We think the Federation might be lying to you about the food simulators being a problem," he interrupted, "or in the least exaggerating the issue. Since you're technically under Federation protection, we can't demand access to you, but we have offered our help. Repeatedly. They won't let us test you for ourselves, and without someone from your city willing to come to the Var palace in secret to let us examine you, we can't prove it one way or another. If they're telling the truth, then we know the food simulators are a bad idea, and we'll take them away. But if they're lying..."

Justina's eyes moved down his body to rest on his clenched fist. She stared at his hand for a moment, and he forced his fingers to loosen.

"What reason do they give you for denying your requests to test us?" Justina kept her eyes downturned and leaned closer as if not wanting to miss his answer.

"They say ESC scientists are investigating their findings, and our primitive medical experience will only sabotage their efforts and expose the population to the very radiation factors they are trying to shield you from. However, if we agree to become an official part of the Alliance, they'll let us see the information we seek. We will never voluntarily join the Alliance."

"Is your medical experience primitive?" she asked.

"My mother was a top scientist working for the ESC when she met my father," he paused to explain, "that's Exploratory Science Commission."

Justina arched a brow. "I know what the ESC is. It's not like we aren't educated. Cysgod was known for its education and technological advances."

"I apologize, my lady. I didn't mean to offend." Roderic hadn't meant to insult her.

She frowned. "You don't have to mock me either."

"I wasn't. I simply meant—"

"Forget it. Please, continue," she said. "We can't stay here much longer. They could send out droids, or some soldier could wander in here to urinate."

"When my mother worked for the ESC, someone had released a compound to genetically

115

alter the vegetation of the shadowed marshes to form a black moss that crept its way underground through the planet's surface to drain the soil of nutrients like a parasite. They called it the Black Crawl. She discovered its source and stopped it. Otherwise, it would have continued to spread and would have killed this entire planet. So, she literally saved this world." Roderic realized he sounded a little defensive and lightened his tone. "Princess Nadja of the Draig is also a scientist. To the north, in Draig territory, there is a low-growing yellow plant whose pollen causes anyone who breathes it in to pass out. Normally, if found, they can be moved and will wake up on their own. However, the problem is when they are not found. They starve to death in their sleep. Nadja developed an inoculation against the deep sleep. Between the two of them, many lives were saved. I trust them to find a better solution for your people."

"What will it matter? For whatever reason, the Federation doesn't want us to have the technology. If they are lying, then they are starving us on purpose. That doesn't change their control over us. Your food simulators don't do us any good sitting in your palace. The Federation won't allow them near the city." She turned his reasoning back on him. "If they're telling the truth, then none of what you're talking about matters."

"Don't you want to know for sure if this radiation scare is true?" he insisted. "We might not be able to stop them, but we can make sure food simulators are near enough to smuggle food rations in."

"What do you mean, near enough?"

Roderic instantly closed the distance between them and lightly touched her arms. "Jaxx, my cousin Payton, and I bought food simulators from space pirates and hid them outside the city while we waited on fuel cells to power them. We have contacts willing to help us distribute."

"What?" She blinked in confusion. "They're near the city?"

"Like you said, we can't set up food simulators in Shelter City because the Federation would find them, but we can deliver food to the city after it's materialized. That was the plan anyway. Before we could finish setting up, this man we call Yellow Shirt got ahold of some of the units. That's what Jaxx and Fiora were doing here. They are trying to find out where he hid them."

"Why are you telling me this?"

"I trust you, and I want you to trust me."

"What if the Federation discovers how you're

interfering with the city? If they find out what you're doing... I thought that would be bad for shifters. Won't they force your hand into a more permanent arrangement? I remember my father and Starrs talking about it when we first arrived."

"It would, but it goes against everything we believe to not interfere. Shifters live by a strong code. If someone is starving, you feed them. If they need a home, you build them shelter. If a child has no family, you make them your family. It's why we said yes when the Federation Military asked to bring you here. We know no other way to live—or we hadn't until that point." Roderic sighed. "We have discussed acquiring portable decontaminators, but there is much more risk of discovery with those."

Justina nodded, seeming to come out of her sorrow a little as they spoke. "If everyone suddenly appeared clean and laundered, they'd know."

"But if extra food rations are passed around, the evidence would quickly be eaten." Roderic gently rubbed her arms a few times before releasing her. He didn't want to let her go, but she didn't ask him to continue. "My mother is fairly certain the food simulators would be harmless. The rations are one of the many ways they control the city into compliance. Let's take some of their power away. If you come with me, we can run tests to be sure."

Justina glanced over her shoulder and then back at him. "I don't..."

"There is a medical booth at the palace." He thought of her kidney. "It will do a comprehensive scan. If there is anything to worry about, it will tell us."

"Medical booth? And they would let me use it?" She glanced down at her clothes. "They'd let me enter the palace even though I'm...like this?"

"We won't tell anyone where you're from. Alien dignitaries visit all the time." Roderic relaxed a little as he saw her determination to return to the city wavering. "If you are returned healthy, isn't that good for Starrs too?"

At that, she gave a small half-smile. "You said you came here as a dignitary?"

Roderic stared at her mouth, happy to see her expression changing. He would do anything to keep that smile on her face. "Yes."

"It shows. You're very manipulative."

He scratched the back of his head in false modesty. "I like to think I'm persuasive."

She brushed her hand against her dirty gown. "I

don't look like a visiting dignitary. I'm...dirty. They'll know."

He began to walk, testing to see if she would fall into step next to him. "Have you ever met a Lophibian? They left slime trails all over the palace floors and stained a guest suite green with their body goo when they were here. Three palace servants slipped the first day of their visit until we blocked the guest hallway from foot traffic."

"*Li-pho-bian?*" she asked. "I've read about them."

"*Lo-phi-bian,*" he corrected. "Confusingly close relation to Liphobians."

Justina hesitated before walking beside him. "So I only have to meet your mother? No one else will know I'm there?"

"I will do everything in my power to protect you. I promise. This is our chance to help your people. Really help."

She took a deep breath and let it out slowly. "Yes. All right. I'll go with you. I'll let your mother do tests on me. I'll use your medical booth. But then I need your word that you will bring me back here as soon as we're done."

"Yes," he agreed against his better judgment. "If that is what you wish."

"It is. Also," she held up a vial, "I need you to tell me what this is and what it will do."

Roderic reached for it and balanced it between two fingers as he held it up to a spot of light coming through the treetops. He didn't recognize the dark liquid. "Where did you get this?"

"From a soldier in the facility. He thought I was someone I wasn't, and I didn't correct him."

Roderic started to pull the cap off the vial.

"Don't." She put her hand over his to stop him. "It might be poisonous."

"What did the soldier tell you to do with it?"

"I'm supposed to drop it on people's food, one drop until the vial is empty, and then they want me to come back for refills." She touched the pouch at her waist. "In return, I get extra food."

He pushed the vial down the top of his boot next to his calf. "That is a strange request."

Justina held out her hand. "Do we have an agreement, prince? Test. Medical booth. Vial. Bring me back. If the food simulators are an option, we'll discuss setting up distribution in the city. We do all that, then your honor debt to Starrs and me is finished. That will more than repay what you feel you owe."

He placed his hand next to hers. "I agree to your

request, but as to the debt, I already told you the gods will let me know when it is repaid."

"That's a deal, prince."

"Call me Roderic."

She nodded and then chuckled. "Fine. Then you may call me my lady. I kind of like the sound of that."

8

JUSTINA TRIED NOT TO COUNT HER STEPS AS they walked away from Shelter City. Thinking about the distance only led to panic. She tried not to contemplate what would happen if Sever realized she never made it down the path or how Starrs would worry when she didn't return. And she really tried not to stare at Roderic and picture him naked as he moved next to her.

The last one was proving to be the most difficult. He moved differently than men in the city. Cysgodians were tense and on edge. Roderic took graceful steps. Though leaves littered the ground, the press of his feet sounded softer than her trampling.

"As a man, you move like when you are a cat," she observed, instantly wishing she could take back the words. Her body wanted to gravitate closer to him, but she remembered the look of disgust on Sever's face when he'd leaned into her. She'd run through the forest, crawled through mud, ripped her dress to bandage a bloody dragon-man, had been knocked around by census drones, and was not given use of a decontaminator. Of course she smelled.

Roderic chuckled. "If you say so."

Justina liked the sound of his voice. It helped to reduce the silence of the trees. In the city, sounds were everywhere, all day and night. She wanted him to keep talking. "Your parents live at the palace?"

Roderic nodded. "They do, as does most of the royal family."

"Most? Have some been exiled?" She ducked under a low branch.

"No. Some have chosen to explore space. Others spend time elsewhere."

"Like you in the forest?"

"My home is in the palace, as is my work when required, but I do prefer the outdoors. They can track me if they need me. My brother, Aybram, is better suited to life as a dignitary than I am."

"You don't enjoy dignitary work?"

"Political conversations are tedious, like a game

no one ever wins for long. It's always searching for what the other person is hiding. I prefer honest conversations, like now with you."

Justina felt pleasure at the way he said the words. She thought of kneeling on the white floor, talking to a stain on her dress. Had something mystical heard her and granted the pain-dazed wish?

"If history quotes me saying anything during my life about my position as a prince, it will be, *'Punching your political opponent for being a slargnot is often not allowed but should be as it is the only path to some satisfaction.'*"

"I'd enjoy punching General Sten," Justina admitted.

"I'd like to do more than punch him," Roderic said. "I want you to know you have friends beyond those city boundaries. We do care what happens to all of you."

"Yes. You said. You bought us food simulators." Justina fought tears. So many times she'd watched dragons flying over them and wondered if they'd all rather just breathe fire and burn down the whole city rather than deal with it. "Thank you for all you are trying to do."

With each pause in the conversation, the soft sounds of the forest took over. Wind rustled the leafy canopies. Their feet brushed along hidden paths between the thick trunks, taking them in a zigzag pattern rather than a straight line. The only thing quieter she could think of was being trapped in the dark tunnel trying to get home.

Worry again filtered through her, tightening her stomach. "If we are separated, how will I know my way home?"

"We won't be."

"How do you know?" she insisted.

"I give you my word." Roderic said it as if that should be the end of her concern on the matter. She wished she had that kind of confidence.

"I should have said something to Starrs. He's going to worry." She slowed her step and glanced back the way they'd come. Trees obstructed any view of the distance. Their canopies blocked the light, so she couldn't guess which direction they moved in by looking for the three suns.

"I will endeavor to get word to him, but if you had gone back, we would've had to risk smuggling you out again." His eyes glanced over her briefly, lingering on her stomach. "I believe we are in a unique situation that we might not get again."

Justina had drawn attention by pulling her stunt with the drones. He was right. The fact she'd been taken would mean her return would garner notice. People would be watching and paying attention.

The quiet returned. Her mind searched for sounds to distract it from deep thought—the familiar shouts of the couple down the street who never had a kind word for each other, of children and their mischief, of men fighting, or a shopkeeper in the marketplace trying to hock her wares.

The sound of leaves crashed together, and she felt the whisper of a breeze stirring her hair. Justina swayed a little as she looked through the trees.

"Are you unwell? Should we rest?" Roderic touched her arm. His hands had a way of gravitating toward her, finding excuses to touch, just like she wanted to lean into him. "I can carry you if you wish."

"I haven't been this far from the city since we arrived," she admitted. "It's all we ever dream about, and yet I find it makes me anxious and dizzy. I keep wondering what the Federation will do when they catch us. It feels like they'll pop out from behind a tree at any moment with a blaster. Or what if someone from the city finds us? The Cysgodian men who sneak into these woods are not to be trusted. They have strange ideas about shifter blood."

"So I have heard." Roderic stepped in a small

circle, searching their surroundings. "They want to eat us and absorb our longevity. Facing mortality causes fear, and that fear triggers irrational beliefs. It's...disturbing."

"I don't think like that."

"I didn't suspect that you did," he assured her. His hand touched her again. The warmth spreading up her arm and making her body tingle with aware-ness. "I can't hear anyone near us. It's safe. It helps if you push those fearful thoughts aside. Concentrate on your next ten steps and where they will take you. Then the next ten."

"Tell me more about your family." She wanted to hear him speak, to have a conversation that had nothing to do with her reality.

"What do you want to know?"

She thought about it for a moment. "What are your parents' names?

"Prince Quinn and Princess Vittoria, but she prefers Tori."

"And the space travelers in your family, are they allowed to leave their royal duties? Or do they get called back to the palace like you are from the forest? Do you all take turns leaving and staying on-world?"

"No, we don't all wish to travel the high skies,"

Roderic answered. "Understanding our way around the universes is valuable, and sometimes it has come in handy to have relatives in space."

"Tell me of an example." Justina wondered what her life would have looked like if her homeworld hadn't been contaminated. If she had been given an education and had been allowed to explore who she wanted to be.

"My Uncle Jarek flew with space pirates for a time. The crew originally belonged to my Aunt Samantha. She was their captain. Sam and her crew were flying by one night. Someone on the ship mistook an alien hallucinogenic drink for liquor. Next morning they woke up to discover they'd kidnapped my Uncle Falke in his shifted form, stuck him in a cell, and were on their way to the Torgan Black Market to sell him."

"So Jarek was in space, and he rescued Falke?"

Roderic's hand slid down to her elbow to steady her as they came to a fallen branch blocking their way. He helped her step over before letting go.

"I've heard different versions of the story, but Jarek's twin brother, Reid, might have been there as well. I know he flew the high skies for a brief period back then," he answered. "Falke ultimately married Samantha. To hear him tell it, his capture was the will of the gods so that he may find his mate. I think there are probably easier ways to make that happen, but Falke seems to like an excuse for why he was taken prisoner so easily by pirates. Jarek absorbed her crew into his, and they got into a little mischief before he met his wife, Mei. Jarek and Mei are in space more than they're home. In fact, Reid and his wife are with them as well."

"And those are the pirates who brought the food simulators?" she concluded.

Roderic nodded. "The same."

"Do you ever go with them? To space, I mean." She looked toward the sky but only saw the green canopy dancing above.

"No. I've been up there before, but ship life is not for me. The VR helps, but I still know I'm in a metal box floating in nothingness." Roderic lifted his arms and took a deep breath. "This is where I belong."

Justina lifted her arms and mimicked his deep breath, trying to feel what he did. "It is a good smell. Whenever I sneak out of the city and come back in, the odors seem stronger. Worse."

Roderic dropped his arms and walked ahead of her. He pushed aside thick underbrush for her to pass through. "There's an easier path through here."

Her gown caught on the brush, pulling the tucked end from her waist. Roderic shook the fabric free for her. She pushed it back into her waist next to the food.

"They gave me these extra rations if you're hungry," she offered.

"Perhaps later. I would like to bring a sample of the food to my mother as well to see where they are getting their supplies. It could provide answers."

"Your mother is an ESC scientist, and several of your elders are space pirates." Justina studied him carefully. She stopped walking as she waited for him to pass through the brush to join her. "I thought royals married other royals."

"Shifters marry who they are meant to be with, whether it is a princess or..." Blue eyes met and held hers. An inner light swirled in their depths. The way his sentence lingered made it difficult for her to take a deep breath. Her heart beat a little faster.

"And how do you know who you are meant to be with?"

"I'm told it's a feeling, a connection." His voice lowered, and his eyes did not waver. "We both wish it, and that is that. Once life mated, it can never be undone. We become connected. There will never be anyone else."

We both? We become?

Her breath caught. Justina recalled what he looked like naked—muscles rippling beneath flesh, strength and sinew, animalistic power. Her throat suddenly felt dry. The first moment she found him stalking toward her on all fours, shifting from animal to man, she'd felt something unusual. Attraction, yes. Roderic embodied all the traits of a passionate Cysgodian fantasy. But there was more.

Or was she imagining it? Hoping for more?

Justina inched away from the intimate turn of the subject. "So what about your king and queen? How did they find each other?"

He seemed disappointed as she again started walking and put distance between them. "King Kirill met his wife, Queen Lyssa, when she came to the planet undercover. She worked for the HIA."

"The queen is an agent for the Human Intelligence Agency?" Justina clarified.

Roderic nodded. "*Was.* My grandfather, before he died, had captured her and put her in...ah..."

"What?" She again stopped as she waited for the answer.

"My grandfather had several half mates. He put her with his wives. He wasn't *with* her before he died." Roderic gave a small laugh. "It's strange. This is the second time today I've discussed King Attor's proclivities."

"Half mates?"

"Wives who are wives but have not been life mated." Roderic gestured toward an opening in the trees. They turned from the woods onto a worn dirt path that made the journey much more convenient. Trees reached over them, providing patches of shade. "A man could have many. Attor had over a hundred."

"A hundred?" Justina repeated in shock. She wondered if Roderic planned on such a thing. "What would a man want with a hundred wives?"

"It's an old practice amongst cat-shifters, and Attor took it to the extreme. He is family and I respect that, but he was also a warmongering egomaniac who had multiple issues. Only a few of the elders still have multiple wives."

"So you aren't, you don't...?"

"Have or want many wives? No. If the gods choose to bless me with a mate, I could not imagine wanting more than one."

"You must have an extensive family." She needed to change the topic. "That must be nice."

"Attor had five children," Roderic said. "They all have children."

"Only five with a hundred wives?" That was surprising.

"The radiation from the blue sun that saves us and gives us long life and health also decreased our birthrates. I think those rates are even lower with half mates, though I can't prove my assumption." Roderic's expression became serious. "I'm sorry you lost your father. What about your mother? Do you have siblings?"

Justina nodded. She didn't want to think of all her losses. There had been so many—family, friends, neighbors.

"Will you tell me about them?"

He'd been forthcoming about his life. She wanted to repay his honesty with her own.

"It's been a long time since I've talked about it." The old pain surfaced as her thoughts turned to the past. "I was a child when our government herded us from our homes. First into medical facilities. There were so many of us that they ran tests by moving us through a long line from room to room. That was where I lost my mother and baby brother to the virus. Next, they brought us into the Federation quarantine facilities, where my father tried to lose himself in his drink. Finally, after people more powerful than we were had agreed to our imprisonment on Qurilixen, they ushered us into cargo ships."

Sure, they hadn't called it prison at the time, but that's what Shelter City had become. A prison.

As a girl, she'd clung to those memories of home. As an adult, she used them as fuel to remind her just how far they had fallen and how hard she needed to fight. Most days, that mind fuel worked. Today wasn't one of those days. Today exhaustion lingered around the tattered edges.

"I was old enough to remember everything that happened to us and too young to understand exactly what it would mean." She traced the edge of the trail with her gaze, staring at where the dirt met yellow grass. "My father brought me here because he didn't have a choice. It was either submit to the Federation's will or death. Sometimes, I think the ones who died from the virus were the lucky ones. They didn't live long enough to see what our people have become. For those younger than me, this will be all they know."

A tear slid down her cheek, and she walked faster.

"When the older generations die off, this is what will be normal, and that breaks my heart," she continued. "And I scream so loud to try to make the others listen. I try to warn them. I see the violence growing in us. I see the violence in them. I see the cyborg and drone presence increasing. I see our shelters falling. I see our children hungry. I see..." She took a shaky breath, gesturing wildly at nothing. "I see..."

Roderic took her by the shoulders, stopping her mounting panic. "See me."

She blinked back tears.

"Look at me. See me." He kept his gaze steady as he cupped her face in his hands. She became trapped in the depths. "This will not last forever. I give you my word. It might not end tomorrow, but it will not be forever."

"It's been a lifetime," Justina whispered.

"I know," he soothed.

He leaned closer and glanced at her mouth as if silently asking permission. His thumb ran along her jawline, sending a tremble of warmth through her. The thoughts swirling in her head stopped as if time held still for them.

Time lost all meaning. Each tickle of his breath on her skin could have been a second or an hour. She pressed her cheek into his palm, nuzzling into his heat. His lips came closer until they parted and hovered near hers. If his eyes asked for permission, she was giving it.

Whoosh-thud!

A blur of movement behind Roderic accompanied the loud sound. Justina screamed and jumped back. She stumbled several steps as she tried to reason through the danger. A dark winged beast blocked the path.

"Dra..." She tried to speak. "Dra-dra-dragon."

She'd seen them in the sky spouting long trails of fire but never had they come this close. At least, not in this form.

Roderic frowned, saying before he had even fully turned around, "Sacred cats, Jaxx!"

A smaller movement came from on top of the dragon.

"Roderic, help me down," Fiora yelled. "I'm still a little shaky from my ordeal."

Roderic glanced at Justina and tried to smile. "It's fine. They're friends."

Justina barely registered what he said. The dragon stared at her. She watched his mouth for fire.

Roderic hurried toward Jaxx and ducked under his wing. When he returned to view, Fiora walked with him. Her stomach looked swollen.

Jaxx tilted his head, still staring.

Justina took a step back.

Fiora reached under her shirt and pulled out a pair of pants. She tossed them on the ground. "Get dressed, my love."

The dragon snorted.

Fiora approached Justina. "You might want to avert your eyes if you're modest. These guys spend half their lives running around naked, so he won't care if you see any dangly bits."

Fiora grinned.

Justina gave a surprised laugh.

Roderic joined them, partially blocking her view of the dragon as the creature began to tremble and shrink. "You look much recovered, Lady Fiora."

Fiora sighed and rubbed her head. "I feel better. Thanks to you." She reached for Justina's shoulder. "Thanks to both of you. Yevgen told me you saved Jaxx's life when you found us help and tied off his wound."

"Anyone would have done the same," Justina answered, leaning to watch the animal shift into a man. When Roderic had shifted, she'd found it sexually appealing. With the dragon, bones popped loudly and made her cringe.

Fiora tilted her head to block her view, not removing her hand from Justina's shoulder. Her grip became firm. "You don't believe that."

"I suppose I don't. But you were always nice to me when we crossed paths. That counts for something." Justina saw the naked Jaxx reaching for his pants and averted her gaze from him. The shifting show had ended.

"I'm sorry. I'm trying, but the visions aren't clear," Fiora said, her voice louder than before. "This is a rare occurrence. Her timeline is veering in multiple directions, like large wiggling tentacles. Decisions need to be made before these timelines settle."

Jaxx joined them, wearing pants and nothing else. "You sounded clear when you woke me up and said we needed to fly here immediately."

"I..." Fiora narrowed her eyes. Her grip became tight.

Justina ignored the pain in her shoulder as the woman's fingers dug into her flesh. She eyed Jaxx warily.

"Is something amiss?" Jaxx touched his face and looked at his wife for help.

"Justina?" Roderic asked.

"Do you breathe fire when you are like this as well?" Justina inquired.

Jaxx chuckled and shook his head in denial. "No, my lady. I'm perfectly harmless."

Fiora eased her grip and laughed. "Harmless? Now that's not true."

Roderic shifted his weight to stand closer to her. Justina relaxed and was finally able to look away from the dragon-man. Fiora used the opportunity to slip out of the woman's hold.

"Did you come to thank her?" Roderic asked.

"No," Fiora said. "But I do thank you, Justina."

Justina nodded.

"We are in your debt—" Jaxx started to add.

"I already assumed the life debts on behalf of the shifters," Roderic inserted quickly. "So she's my responsibility. I'll take care of her."

Jaxx arched a brow, and his lip curled at the side. "Fiora, my love, does this mean what I think it means?"

"If you think it means Roderic wants to claim Justina as a bride, then yes." Fiora nodded. "That is definitely one of the timeline options I'm seeing. That decision would settle the timelines."

Jaxx grinned at Roderic.

Roderic lifted his finger and pointed in warning. "Jaxx, I'm cautioning you."

"My love?" Jaxx's smile widened. "What timeline would have happened if—?"

"If you hadn't interrupted with your landing?" Fiora finished. "They'd be having dirt sex."

Justina coughed in surprise at the blunt prediction. "No, I mean..." She glanced at Roderic for confirmation, or maybe to make the conversation stop. She wasn't sure which route she wanted this moment to take.

Suddenly Fiora gasped. "I see the danger now." She grabbed Justina's arm and pulled her to the trees. "We need to go."

Jaxx swiped his shirt from the path as Roderic moved with Justina to the trees.

Fiora pointed at the ground. "Lie down. Don't make a sound."

Roderic automatically obeyed the command. He pulled Justina's wrist, making her join him on the forest floor. Soft leaves and one very bothersome twig made her bed.

"We're not having sex here, like this," Justina protested. She wasn't getting naked with the other couple so close.

"Shh," Fiora warned, her eyes wide with fear. She laid on her stomach. Jaxx jumped into the trees from the path and landed on all fours as he crouched over his wife.

Roderic placed the flat of his fingers against Justina's lips as he settled his body next to hers. He leaned up and strained his neck to look out from their hiding spot. For a long moment, nothing seemed to happen.

Justina heard the soft tap of muffled footsteps. They gradually became louder. Fiora stared at her, shaking her head as if to warn her not to do what she might do. Justina bit back her urge to ask who was coming.

She looked at Roderic's strong neck stretching above her. A pulse beat thumped a stable rhythm, much calmer than the pounding in her chest. She opened her mouth to take a deeper breath from beneath his fingers covering her lips.

Even as the sound of the footsteps retreated, they continued to hide. She felt the press of his body against her length, felt his heat and each subtle shift of muscle. Closing her eyes, she let the acute awareness of his nearness comfort her. With Roderic, she felt safe.

9

"DID SHE FALL ASLEEP IN THE MIDDLE OF...?" Jaxx looked at where Justina rested on the ground and then at Roderic.

"She's had a trying day," Roderic defended. He held out his hand. "Toss me the shirt."

Jaxx threw his shirt.

Roderic caught it and gently tucked it under Justina's head. She made a soft sound in her sleep but did not open her eyes. He wanted to touch her cheek again, to go back to that moment before Jaxx had landed.

"Fiora? Would you...?" Roderic motioned toward Justina. Fiora nodded and sat on the ground next to her. "How is she? Can you see her future at all?"

Fiora pinched the top of her nose and closed her eyes. "I'm sorry, no. It's still unclear."

Roderic moved out of the trees to the path. Jaxx joined him, and they stared at where the group of marsh farmers had disappeared. If he concentrated, he could hear the soft press of paws moving cautiously. Deep ruts cut into the earth from the sleigh they dragged behind them. The smell of liquor lingered in the air.

"Did we interrupt more than sex with our landing?" Jaxx's tone was light, but there was also concern in his expression.

"No."

Jaxx chuckled. "I don't believe you."

"It was a good thing you interrupted."

"Fiora insisted we find you," Jaxx said. "She wasn't certain what the danger was, but I think a gathering of drunk marsh farmers hauling an unsanctioned still through the woods counts as a threat."

"I am ashamed to admit my concentration was elsewhere," Roderic admitted.

"Ashamed? What a strange word to choose. Though I guess we've both acted foolish when it comes to women. I was attacked because of my wife's ass." Jaxx patted him on the shoulder before going to kick at the deep rut. "The marsh farmers step lightly, but they're not very stealthy, are they? They left us a trail right to them."

"Drunken men make poor decisions," Roderic agreed. He thought of Justina's mouth, so close to his. "As do sober ones."

"Talk to me," Jaxx urged, striking the sides of the rut to bury a small section as if by doing so he could right the walkway they'd destroyed.

"She has a man. Apparently, he is large and likes to bite off ears." Roderic frowned.

Jaxx scrunched his brow and started to laugh but then stopped. "You cannot be serious."

"She told me."

"That's not..." Jaxx frowned and walked toward the women. "Fiora, love, does Justina have a man who bites off ears?"

"Not that I've ever seen in any of my encounters with her timeline," Fiora whispered. Though her voice was soft, Roderic heard her easily. "I don't know her to have any lovers. She spends much of her time with her neighbor, but they are not intimate in that way."

Jaxx rejoined him. "I don't know why she told you that, but she has no man."

The news filled Roderic with hope, only to have

reality instantly dash it. As a Cysgodian, Justina might as well be light years away from him. They couldn't be together. They weren't even supposed to know each other. Perhaps that was why Justina had lied about it, to keep him away from her, to make it easier for the both of them.

And she was right to do so. He knew that. Too many lives were entwined in this mess.

"Life has become complicated, has it not?" Jaxx mused. "Do you ever think about when we were young before the Federation came and took the focus from all else in our lives? Sometimes I start to forget what it was like to not have that knot of worry. Do you remember those secret camping trips we thought our parents never knew about, where we would meet and pretend that we were being indoctrinated into an ancient secret shifter society, and we needed to perform tasks to be members?"

Roderic laughed. They had been foolish dares that ended more than once in scrapes and bruises. "Why was it we Var were always dared to go up into the sky with you Draig?"

Jaxx laughed. "I don't know who panicked more. The cat in the air, or the people on the ground when it rained vomit."

"That was because you flung us in circles as you

dove. Don't think I've forgotten I still owe you for that horror." Roderic gave a tiny shiver of repulsion. "If those childhood adventures taught me anything, it is that my feet belong firmly on the ground. Or at the very highest, a sturdy tree limb."

"Didn't you already get your revenge when you made me drink that—*what was it?*—dark Earth stuff from the food simulator."

"Black coffee," Roderic chuckled.

"Ugh, yes. I still have nightmares about that bitter taste." Jaxx flicked his tongue as if he could still recall it even decades later. "It had me flying in frantic circles for an hour. I thought my heart might explode."

"Who would have known all that sneaking around was preparing us for Shelter City?"

"Our parents knew," Jaxx said. "My father admitted as much years later."

Roderic laughed harder. "I'm not surprised. I can't believe we honestly thought half the shifter royal children could disappear for a night without anyone noticing."

"But they never stopped us. They let us pretend," Jaxx said. "I've been thinking about our youth lately, of what it must have been like for our parents to trust us in the woods running around like a wild pack of animals. It won't be the same for our children, will it?"

Roderic's eyes widened, and he looked toward where the women were hidden. A smile began to spread over his features. "Is Fiora with child?"

Jaxx shook his head in denial. "No, but someday, with the gods' blessing."

Roderic thought of what it might be like to be a father. It wasn't something he'd considered, being unattached, but now that thought instantly led him to think about Justina.

"I want them to have the childhood we were given. Not safeguarded like our parents growing up during the shifter wars. How can we teach our sons about honor when Shelter City is allowed to remain standing as it is?"

"Maybe you'll have a daughter," Roderic offered.

The thought didn't comfort his friend. Jaxx appeared terrified by the idea of raising a girl. Considering the mischief their female cousins had caused, Roderic couldn't say he blamed him. Men liked to believe women needed protection—and perhaps that once had been true when alien women came to marry a male population filled with talons and claws. So it stood to reason, what could be more delicate than a daughter? But a shifter girl? She defied and frustrated that instinct and their fierce ways were enough to test the courage of any father.

"Should we track the marsh farmers and confiscate their still?" Jaxx asked.

"Normally, that would make for a fun diversion, but we need to get Justina to the palace." Roderic turned his attention to the women, picking up on the soft breath of Justina's breathing as she rested. "She needs a medical booth."

"Is she injured?" Jaxx asked.

Roderic told Jaxx about what had happened to her after the drones dropped her off at the facility and what he'd overheard when he'd been ready to save her. Jaxx listened, quietly nodding at intervals. When he finished, Roderic reached into his boot and pulled out the vial. "The man gave her this liquid and told her to put drops in the food of other Cysgodians. From what I gather, if she does it, he'd let her use the medical booth. If she doesn't, whatever is ailing her will kill her."

"What is this?" Jaxx took the vial and examined it.

"I don't know. I'm hoping my mother might be able to tell us." Roderic again listened for Justina, comforted by the sound of her breathing. "After the medical booth, I have to take her back to the city before they discover she left. I promised her."

"Roderic, I'm sorry." Jaxx sadly shook his head. "She's—"

Roderic held up his hand, not wanting to hear the words out loud. He knew what he felt was impossible.

"You know when you show up with her at the palace, our elders are going to know we've been going into the city," Jaxx said. His parents knew what they were doing, but they were the only ones they spoke to about it. "There are going to be questions. You need to prepare how much you want to answer."

Roderic arched a brow. "You think they don't already suspect?"

Jaxx grinned. "Just like when we were children, they let us think we're getting away with something? We don't tell? They don't ask?"

"Jaxx! Take off your pants! I see one of her possible timelines." Fiora rushed from her hiding spot.

Roderic frowned and lifted his hands toward Jaxx in protest. "Now, wait—"

"Justina needs a medical booth. Now!" Fiora went to her husband and tugged at his pants to get them off. "You need to fly all three of us to the Var palace." She glanced at Roderic. "Get her."

Roderic was already on his way to where Justina slept. He kneeled beside her and gently touched her face. "Justina? Wake up. We need to go."

She moaned softly. Her skin had paled with sickness. Roderic took her into his arms and carried her. Panic caused his heart to race.

"I know you want to run, but it's too far," Fiora warned. Jaxx shifted into dragon form, and she instantly climbed onto his back. Fiora closed her eyes before saying, "Give him Justina's wrist. It's the only way. If we put her on his back, she'll fall off. I can't hold her and keep my own grip."

Roderic did as she commanded. Jaxx took hold of Justina with a talon.

"Hold up your arm and shut your eyes," Fiora commanded. "This is going to be a hellish ride."

The irony was not lost on him that they'd just been discussing this very horror.

"If anything happens and you can't support all of us. Drop me," Roderic told Jaxx.

Jaxx spouted flames upward in a short burst.

"I'm holding you to that," Roderic said, lifting his arm.

As Jaxx beat his wings and lifted up into the

air, Roderic bit back his apprehension. He normally didn't have a problem with heights if he was at the top of the palace or one of the watchtowers where his feet had solid footing. If evolution had decided anything, it was that cats were not meant to fly.

His fear of flying was heavily outweighed by his concern for Justina. Jaxx lifted her from the ground by her arm. She dangled unconsciously. Roderic willed her eyes to stay closed, even as he wanted her to wake up to tell him she was all right.

Jaxx's taloned fist clamped around his wrist, and Roderic wrapped his fingers around the dragon's leg. Before Jaxx lifted him off the ground, he reached for Justina's hand and held it, hoping to steady her. His heart beat hard as he stared at her. As much as he wanted to carry her and run, dragon flight was faster.

"Go!" Roderic yelled.

Jaxx's wings pumped as he lifted them above the path to hang over the treetops. His grip stayed tight. Higher up, the air became cold, and the sound of it rushing past his ears distorted his hearing. They passed the point where a fall would mean broken bones to where there would be no survival. And still, they climbed higher.

Jaxx thrust forward, moving faster. The landscape blurred beneath them.

Roderic didn't look at their dangling feet. He stared at Justina. Their bodies angled back like the banners decorating the palace in a windstorm. He felt as helpless as that fluttering material, kept anchored by one hand. Each flap of the wings undulated their bodies. His joints strained—shoulder, elbow, wrist—under the weight of his body.

Roderic tightened his grip on Justina's hand. Her body temperature chilled faster than his. He trusted his friend, but he needed to protect her. If Jaxx's grip slipped, Roderic would be there to catch her.

Justina opened her eyes. Roderic tensed, holding tighter in case she panicked. Her eyes rolled slightly before closing once more. Thankfully, she had not seen him.

Roderic focused on his breathing and on her face. Her lips parted, and he tried to hear the sound of each intake of air, but it became impossible to differentiate it from the wind.

Jaxx turned, and their bodies tilted with his flight. What would have taken them days to walk at a human pace had been reduced to an hour, give or take, but it felt like an eternity.

Jaxx turned again, and the flapping blue banners of the Var palace came into view. The imposing walls of the castle had stood for hundreds of years, crafted to withstand an attack. It dominated the surrounding forest and Var city nestled in the valley below.

Since shifters lived for hundreds of years, they'd had time to perfect their trades, which showed in the carefully placed tile work. The designs created complex symmetrical patterns of blue, red, orange, gold, and green. Arched entryways were carved by hand, but some of the exterior engravings had begun to show wear from the elements. Roderic saw a few of the craftsmen repairing an old doorway in the turret. Those same master craftsmen had most likely installed the doors in their youth.

Jaxx slowed as he brought them over a flat roof extension of the palace meant for docking spaceships. It was not the stealthy entrance Roderic initially had planned. People would be watching, and word would spread, but none of that mattered now.

Roderic kicked his feet in anticipation of the landing. Jaxx released him a few feet above the stone. Roderic dropped and instantly reached to catch Justina around the waist. When he had her supported, Jaxx let go of her.

Roderic ignored the dizziness in his head as he held her cold body against his warmer one. He heard a shout come down from one of the stone turrets but couldn't make out the words. His complete attention was focused on Justina. He carried her across the platform. The reinforced steel door leading into the palace was closed.

"What are they saying?" Fiora asked.

"A ship is landing. We have to get inside," Jaxx answered, just as a red light glowed from above. He ran naked past Roderic to slam his fist against the metal door. The air heated, and the wind picked up to whip their hair around their heads. Jaxx pulled Fiora in front of him to block her with his body as the ship came closer.

Roderic kicked at the door as he held Justina, banging as loud as he could. She flopped in his arms, completely unaware of what happened. "Let us in!"

The door slid open, and Roderic rushed Justina inside. Fiora and Jaxx joined them.

"What were you doing out there?" Princess Samantha hit the scanner with the flat of her hand to close the door behind them as the visiting spaceship continued to dock. Her blonde hair was streaked with a purple shade that matched her eyes. She looked them over in concern, not caring about the fact Jaxx stood naked after his shift. "Roderic? Jaxx? What's happened? Who is—?"

Roderic saw his aunt's expression change as she looked at Justina's attire.

"Why do you have a Cysgodian woman with you?" Samantha demanded. "What's going on?"

"She needs a medical booth," Roderic answered.

"Take her to the family unit near the tiger tapestry next to my home," Samantha ordered, ushering him to move. "Then stash her in the blue suite. I'll get the codes to reset the unit once I'm done greeting the dignitaries. No one must know she's here. Jaxx, Fiora, go with him and make sure she's not seen."

"Yes, princess," Jaxx responded.

"Lovely to see you again, Fiora," Samantha said, her tone calm as she went to intercept a guard coming out of the control booth.

Roderic rushed down the hall, taking a quick succession of turns. During the wars, the halls were designed as mazes so those unfamiliar with the palace would become easily trapped. He heard Jaxx and Fiora running to keep up with him, and he also heard when they took a wrong turn and had to correct themselves.

The sound of heavy boots made Roderic dart into a small inlet. Seconds later, Jaxx ran past him, uttering, "On it."

Fiora ducked into the inlet next to him.

"Best I don't get asked questions," Fiora said. "I'll confess everything."

Roderic nodded.

"Prince Jaxx? I didn't know you were visiting. Did Payton hide your clothes again?" Prince Falke often sounded gruff and exasperated. It was understandable considering he'd been the Var Commander since the wars. Even with the reputation, Roderic knew his uncle to be a man who would do anything for his family.

"I came to see if Ryland has pants I could borrow," Jaxx said.

"He's off-world again, but I believe Hunt will have something you can use," Falke answered. "Come, let's see if we can locate his wardrobe."

Roderic listened for his uncle's footsteps while staring at Fiora.

A door opened and closed. Roderic made a move to leave. Fiora grabbed his arm and shook her head. Roderic paused. Silence stretched before another pair of footsteps passed. As the sound lessened, she nodded for him to go.

Roderic ran past the large tapestry filled with cat-shifter warriors led by a giant white tiger that depicted Falke in his shifted form. The medical room door sensed his nearness and opened.

"Turn it on," he said as he laid Justina on the booth and pulled the lid down to trap her inside. He glanced through the narrow opening to watch as green lasers illuminated her body from within.

"We made it in time to help her," Fiora said, even before the machine had time to scan Justina. "But it's going to take a while. I can hide out in here with her if you need to—"

"No," Roderic denied. "I'm not leaving her."

He went to check the console for himself. Satisfied that Fiora had set the unit to do a full scan, he sat on the floor next to Justina to be close to her. Fiora's prediction about making it on time gave him some comfort on a logical level but seeing Justina unconscious filled him with a type of fear no amount of assurances could ease.

10

"AND YOU BROUGHT HER HERE?" A WOMAN asked.

Justina heard the voice from far away. She kept her eyes closed. Her mind drifted in the fog between waking and sleep, and she couldn't pull apart what was real from dreams. Her body felt as if she were carried by drones, but her mind focused on the conversation.

"It was a life debt," Roderic's voice answered. The sound of it pulled her from the torturous flight of the drones toward the safety she felt near him. "Because of her Jaxx and Fiora live."

"You did as honor commanded, my son," a man said, though he didn't seem pleased, "and we will all have to face the price."

Roderic's father, Prince Quinn?

"Calm yourself, my love," the woman admonished. "You are the one who instilled honor in our son. You can't be angry when he only acts as you have instructed."

Princess Tori, his mother.

"I'm not angry. I'm concerned," Quinn said.

"He was right to bring her." Tori's words were followed by soft tapping and a series of beeps. "Her body is riddled with growths. Even first-generation medical scanners would pick these up. How do you know her?"

"She brought Princess Fiora to me in the forest," Roderic said. "Then she saved Jaxx by sacrificing herself to a couple of census drones."

"Drone blasters wouldn't cause this," his mother said. "This is long-term damage and easily treatable, time consuming but easy."

"The Federation just scanned her." Roderic sounded farther away. "I don't know all the details, but they mentioned she might start to urinate blood."

"Probably the mass on her kidney," Tori stated. "I'll know more when I see the full report."

"Is it an effect of the virus?" his father asked.

"Or the radiation poisoning they've been adamant about?"

"The Federation hasn't been forthcoming with the medical records, but if the radiation poisoning claims are true, I would expect this medical booth to cause the abnormalities to worsen. Instead, the lasers are working." Tori sounded irritated. "Their doctors should have been able to help her."

Justina felt as if something warm brushed her cheek. She wondered if it was Roderic's fingers caressing her.

"Her brain activity is showing she's waking up," his mother said over a series of beeps. "She's going to be in there for hours. Let's make sure she rests comfortably. No need to—"

"Justina? Can you hear me?"

Justina fought to open her eyes and turned her head to follow Roderic's voice.

"Justina?" He sat next to her, lower than where she rested, so his shoulders were on level with her eyes. He leaned over so she could see his face. "It's good to see you with us. You've been asleep for quite some time."

"I think I hear your parents?" She lifted her head only to bump it on the top of the booth. "Ow."

Lasers instantly danced over her head where she'd bumped it, soothing the irritation.

"They were here earlier. They stepped out for a few hours while the booth works." He smiled as if relieved. She stared at his mouth, liking the expression. "I don't want you to worry. The booth is doing what it's supposed to do."

"The masses?" She moved her hands to touch her stomach.

"Removed. We kept you asleep while the booth excised them."

"They're going to know I did something if they look again and I'm cured," Justina protested.

"We're not putting the masses back," Roderic answered.

"Isn't there something harmless you can implant that will look like—"

A door slid open, interrupting her.

"How is our guest?" his mother's voice asked. Tori leaned next to Roderic. She had kind, dark eyes. "You look much better. I'm Tori."

"Justina," Justina answered.

"She wants us to put something harmless in her to disguise the fact the masses were removed," Roderic said.

"Well, that's one idea." Tori stood and walked

away. Beeping started. Moments later, Tori returned to look at her. "Justina, how long have you had the tracker?"

"I don't carry a tracker." Justina frowned.

"Tracker implant," Tori clarified.

Justina shook her head in denial. "I don't..."

"It's in your back cheek." Tori gestured toward Justina's ass. "And it looked as if your body was allergic to the alloy used, and that's why you passed out."

Justina remembered the painful injection she'd received while in the Federation facility. "Sever had me in the medical booth."

"Who's Sever?" Roderic asked.

"I told you about him. The Federation soldier who gave me..." Justina suddenly found it hard to breathe. "If they put a tracker in me, they know I'm not in the city. They'll know you helped me. I... Starrs!"

"Is she talking about the man who gave her the vial?" Tori asked.

Roderic nodded. "Sever."

"Let me out of here," Justina insisted. "I need to get back before it's too late."

"I'm afraid it is already far too late. If they are monitoring you, they already know you left the city and came here." Tori stood. "I have to tell the family to expect a visit from General Sten."

"What do you think they'll do?" Roderic asked.

"Starrs," Justina insisted.

"I don't know. Try to avoid Federation residency?" Tori sighed heavily. "But I know what I need to do. As soon as she's done, send me her entire report. Don't let Sam delete it from the machine. Her first instinct will be to hide all the evidence of Justina being here. There is no point trying to hide her now. I'm going to analyze the vial and the food she brought with her. Hopefully, there is something in there we can leverage. Tell me, is there any chance they know about the food simulator you've been trying to smuggle in?"

Roderic cleared his throat.

"You used Sam's old crew. Like they weren't going to mention it to us?" Tori gave a short laugh.

"I don't know what they know," Roderic said.

"Roderic, I need to go back for Starrs." Justina tried to push her way out of the booth. She hated feeling trapped.

"Is there anything else that might come up when we talk to the general?" Tori insisted.

"Turn this off. I need to leave." Justina pushed harder, pressing up with her knee.

"We can't let you do that," Tori said. Again she heard the tapping fingers on the console then beeps as the computer worked. "First, we need to remove the tracker. Then I need extra samples of your blood and tissue sent to my lab."

"I promise, we'll do everything we can for Starrs. I think your staying here is the best hope he has." Roderic reached into the booth to push back her hair. "If you return and they catch you with him, they might think he had something to do with your escape as well."

"Roderic, get your hand out of there," Tori ordered. "Your bruises are interfering with the lasers."

Roderic withdrew his hand.

"You don't have to do this. Tell the Federation I ran away. Tell them I came here on my own, confused, and as soon as you realized who I was, you sent me back." Justina again tried to force her way out of the medical booth. The console buzzed in warning. "Tell them about my allergy. Tell them it affected my brain, and I was confused, but I'm better now. Tell them I was too dirty and you didn't see the markings on my temple until after you cleaned me up."

"They won't believe it unless you can fly."

Roderic shook his head in denial. His eyes disappeared from view as he glanced toward where the console would be. She couldn't see it from her angle. "Jaxx gave us a lift when you were passed out. They're going to know you moved too fast to do it on your own."

"I agree. She's in the cat shifter palace and moved at a speed only dragons could naturally travel. They'll ask why she was brought here and not to the Federation who was closer." Tori sighed, sounding slightly overwhelmed and distracted. "Looks like Jaxx is going to be notifying his family as well. I'll let your father know to expect the Draig royals. With the Shandrot and Nenarraten ships arriving today, we'll have a full palace. Especially when the latter insists on touching anything shiny, which reminds me to tell you not to wear your crown to any ceremonies. Things went missing the last time they were here. Too bad it's not the Syog, but they won't be here for another month. If the Federation attacks, they'd be up for fighting anyone. The Nenarraten will probably try to blind them with reflective jewelry before plucking shiny bits off their uniforms."

"I think Jaxx is with Falke," Roderic said.

"Send the results and samples when this

finishes. Don't let me forget that I need to cancel my trip to the shadow marshes to take the annual soil samples. There are regions not recovering as well as I had hoped." Tori abruptly left to the sound of the door sliding open and shut in quick succession.

"I'm sorry." A tear slipped over Justina's cheek. Her view of him was narrow, but she couldn't look away. She tried to reach her fingers out to him, but the booth was too confining. She didn't care if it slowed the scans, she wanted to touch him. "This is not what I wanted. I never wanted to be a burden or cause a war."

"This is not your doing. You're here because I begged you to come with me. Something had to happen to end this deadlock we have with the Federation. Things cannot go on like this." Roderic reached his hand in to meet hers. Their fingers twined in gentle, tiny movements, and their eyes locked.

Justina felt their connection. The perfect silence of it swept into her soul, an undercurrent beneath the hum of the medical booth and the threat of the Federation. This feeling had to be the opposite of endless darkness.

"You're not a dreamless dream devoid of pain," she whispered.

"I'm...?" He furrowed his brow. "Are you saying I'm...painful?" He withdrew his hand. "Am I hurting you?"

Justina realized what she'd said and how badly it sounded out of context. "When my mother died, my father told me that death was this swirling vortex of darkness that pulled you in. He called it a dreamless dream devoid of pain. The thought of nothingness has terrified me since I was a child. Without pain, there is no joy."

"So I'm not a dreamless dream devoid of pain," he said, his hand returning to hold hers. His lip curled up at the corner. "The booth might have given you something for the discomfort as it removes the tracker."

Justina tried to keep her thoughts from scattering.

"You're endless light, like the suns that constantly shine on this planet. There's pain here, but there has to be because there would not be fleeting moments of beauty that make the journey worth it without it. I haven't always realized that, but it's true, right?" Her eyes closed briefly as she remembered the forest as he stood naked when they first met. Every detail remained clear. "Sunlight trickling overhead through a canopy of leaves.

That's what I feel when I look at you. Little dancing lights piercing the darkness."

"I feel dancing lights when I look at you as well." He caressed her cheek.

Justina laughed. "I think those are the lasers."

His touch sent shivers over her. "I think it's you."

"I feel as if I've known you longer than a day." She rubbed her face against his hand.

"That's because you have known me for three." He gave light taps on her jawline as he counted and said, "One, we met in the forest, and that evening I saved Jaxx. Two, yesterday you were released by Sever, and we came here. Three, today."

"Sometimes it's hard to follow the light, and I lose track of the hours." She frowned. "I've been in this booth that long?"

Roderic nodded. "You needed to sleep through several of the surgeries. It was the only way to remove the tumors."

"You've been here every time I open my eyes. Did you go home to rest?" Justina felt pressure along her backside, and the machine removed the tracker. It was then she realized she couldn't move her leg.

He nodded toward the ground. "The floor in here is quite comfortable."

"Our entire time together has been running or me unconscious," she whispered, closing her eyes. Justina concentrated on the soft caress of his fingers.

"And still I know," he answered.

She meant to ask him what he knew, but the words faded into a dream.

11

A CLEAN DRESS AND HEALTHY, decontaminated body could not mask the insecurity Justina felt standing before the imposing royal families. One of his cousins, Payton, had given her a gown to wear. The yellow embroidered material hung loose on her frame and was more elegant than anything found in Shelter City. It had been a kind gesture, but the ill fit reminded her of how she didn't belong. The color also didn't flatter her complexion.

Life was certainly different on this side of the planet.

Roderic's parents, Quinn and Tori, sat in the great banquet hall next to catshifter royals Falke, Samantha, King Kirill and Queen Lyssa. Joining them were the dragon royals, Jaxx, Prince Grier, and

Grier's parents King Ualan and Queen Rigan, and Jaxx's aunt and uncle, Princess Nadja and Prince Olek. There were others, but she'd already forgotten their names.

Roderic stood in front of the kings and queens with his back to her, leaving her to wait alone. Justina silently ran through the list of names she could remember, not wanting to forget should they speak directly to her. In truth, she didn't know what to expect. Her meager life experiences could not do justice to what it felt like to be in the Var palace.

She remembered the old buildings from her homeworld, tall shiny structures that looked like wet glass—clean and pure—towering over her small body. Though it was possible her childhood amongst decaying metal had morphed reality into a glamour-ized wish for the past. The giant facility towering over Shelter City was grand in scale, but the squared corners and bland white corridors could not compete with the Var palace's arched doorways and high domed glass ceilings that diffused the light of the three suns.

Beneath the domes, strips of gauzy material flowed from the center of the ceiling and anchored to the walls. It showcased a long table where the royals sat high on a platform and faced the main dining hall floor. Though the sea of tables they presided over was empty, she could imagine what it would be like when the room was packed. The family would be on display, marking their authority in clothes that had not been repaired with jagged patchwork. Clean hands would lift food to mouths that had not known the devastating slap of hunger.

She'd read stories of nobility and various ways that leaders acted, but none of those stories helped her now. Some cultures bowed, others laid on their stomachs, others turned their backs, and some threw punches as signs of respect. Justina did none of those things. She stood, knees locked and legs stiff, as she tried to control her trembling.

When she turned her attention from the ceiling back to the family, she saw that many of them stared at her. Their expressions ranged from curious to upset, though none appeared hostile about her attendance. Only two looked at her with pity. Tori passed a handheld device to Nadja, and both women kept glancing at her and shaking their heads as they engaged in whispered conversation.

"The Nenarraten will take her for a price," Samantha said. "Or I could call in favors. Rick is always up for mischief. He and Dev are not afraid to spit into the eyes of the Federation. They'll protect her and take her anywhere she wants to go. The Federation can't prove she was here if they can't find her."

Justina shook her head as she inched closer to the table. "I can't leave."

If she did, where would she go? There was not a home waiting for her. Her skills were limited to hauling carts, repairing homes that should have fallen over decades ago, and digging secret tunnels.

If the royals heard her protest, they didn't respond.

"She can travel under Roane identification," Falke added, nodding at his wife. "We'll say she was a distant cousin visiting from my mother's family."

"I can't leave," she repeated louder.

Roderic turned, and all eyes found her at the same time. She averted her gaze nervously.

"I have family. Starrs. I can't leave my people." Her voice was not as strong as she wanted, and her hands visibly shook. With the Federation, she knew what to expect. She knew which actions would have consequences. Here, she didn't know the proper way to behave. What she did know was that she couldn't leave Starrs behind. "Roderic, you promised we'd help Starrs."

"Starrs?" King Kirill repeated. "What do you mean by that?"

"Her family," Roderic explained. "He's in Shelter City."

"If my son gave his word, we'll do what we can to get Starrs out," Quinn said. "We'll try to get him to you after you're settled in your new homeworld."

"No." Justina again shook her head. "I'm not leaving without him. Besides, we have nowhere else to go. I know the risks here. What's to say another planet will be better? My people are here. I belong with them. I will not abandon them to fight the Federation without me."

Her eyes met Roderic's. There were other reasons she didn't want to be banished from the planet, but they were not reasons she could contemplate. Even though every fiber of her being pulled in his direction, begging to be closer to him, that was not their reality. When they met, she hadn't been lying when she said their stories came from two very different books. This palace and these royals made that difference abundantly clear.

"This is not up for debate, my lady," Falke stated. "We cannot protect you from the Federation without starting a war."

"Cannot or will not? I'm owed a life debt,"

Justina insisted, unsure if this was her best course of action. "Two, in fact, I can't imagine banishment is how your gods would demand you repay it."

Jaxx's lip curled up in a half-smile that he tried to hide from his family. He gave her a slight nod of approval.

"No one is saying banishment," Falke answered.

"How else am I to see being sent away against my will? If you send me away, then how will I collect? Can you guarantee my safety in the high skies?" She turned to King Ualan, who had sat quietly watching. "I saved your dragon's life and his wife. Starrs did too. We're owed considerations. If you don't want to offer protection, then send me back. I can take care of myself."

"It is as she says," Jaxx supported her statements, coming to stand on her left. "I would be dead without their help. As would Fiora."

"Rarely have I seen such bravery. I have taken responsibility for the life debts on behalf of both families," Roderic added, coming to stand at her right. He placed his hand on her shoulder, the act oddly possessive. It sent a small shiver down her back. "Then, subsequently, after drones attacked her and flew her into the stronghold where she was threatened and mistreated by one of the soldiers, she still agreed to come here and help us defeat the Federation at great danger to herself. She's brought us intel on what they're up to—not only in her medical scans my mother has but in her food rations and the vial she's willingly given us for evaluation."

Justina took a deep breath. Her hands still shook, but she pushed past the nerves. "My homeworld is dead. I know you don't recognize the Cysgodian population as anything more than guests, but I have lived here longer than I did on my birth planet. My people are here, and I don't want to leave while they are still trapped under the tyranny of the Federation. I have heard much about shifter honor, and I hope you can respect my feelings on this matter."

To her surprise, Falke nodded. "I concede to your argument. You will not be sent from Qurilixen."

"Thank you, Prince Falke." Justina shook off Roderic's hand as she stepped forward. She met each of their gazes as she implored them to understand. "The truth is, we're your neighbors, and we're not doing well. The hopelessness has long set in and taken root. I know you've had issues with men attacking outside the borders, and I'm sure you're aware of the rhetoric against shifters. All of that is born of desperation and frustration. Those men do not represent the entire city." She felt tears lining her eyes and swiped them away. "We just want a chance to be what we once were. To teach our children. To work. To love. To breathe free. To eat a meal."

"That is not too much to ask," Queen Lyssa said. "We wish the same for you."

"They're about to cut our food rations again," Justina explained. "We have no room for crops, and we can't leave to hunt or forage. We are at the mercy of those rations."

Tori stood from the table and brought her hand-held toward King Kirill. "Look at her scans."

The banquet hall became quiet as they passed the handheld amongst themselves. Queen Lyssa swore softly under her breath. Queen Rigan covered her mouth and shook her head.

After a long moment, Kirill asked, "How often do they feed you now?"

"Rations are given every three days," Justina answered.

"But those rations are not three days' worth of meals," Tori insisted. "Those are not the levels of someone who eats on a daily basis. In fact, I'm recommending supplement shots to help with bone density. The booth was able to rebuild some of the muscle damage, but she'll need more treatments."

"That level of food distribution does not line up with the reports we're given," Rigan stated. "And if this scan is any indication, the health reports are just as fictional."

"That is evidence of their lies, right here." Nadja gestured at the handheld and then toward Justina. "This will not stand. I'd like to see the rest of the data, Tori, if you wouldn't mind?"

"I have been counting on your help," Tori answered.

Justina slowly backed up to stand between Jaxx and Roderic again. Roderic's hand brushed against the back of hers, not taking it but simply touching it as if to let her know he was with her.

"Rigan, I'd like to see those health reports as far back as you have," Nadja said. "My father used to modify his reports. There is one thing I know about criminal behavior. They tend to get lazy. Patterns will emerge if you know where to look for them."

"Of course." Rigan pushed up from her chair. "I'll contact the palace and have Kane send them immediately."

Rigan strode for the banquet hall doors and left.

"If anyone needs us, we'll be in my laboratory."

Tori motioned for Nadja to come with her as they followed Rigan out. "Direct our meals there."

Justina watched the women leave. To Roderic, she quietly asked, "Is Nadja's father part of the Federation?"

Jaxx answered for him, leaning close to her ear. "He was a boss in the Medical Mafia. She came to one of the bridal ceremonies to escape him."

Justina glanced at him to determine if he was joking.

"All true," Jaxx said.

"Jaxx, I hate to ask this of your wife, but has she mentioned anything that might help us?" Grier inquired. Justina recognized him from the city. He'd been there several times with a woman who looked like Fiora.

"The multiple timelines are not coming clearly to her since we left Shelter City," Jaxx said. "She's been in the medical booth, and she's sleeping right now in the blue suite. I left her with her sister."

"What I was trying to—" Justina began.

"Come in." Kirill lifted his hand and waved forward.

Justina started to walk toward him when she noticed they all looked at the door. A guard came into the hall, moving around the table to whisper to the king.

Kirill frowned. "A fleet of Federation transports has been spotted in the forest. They have not sent advance notice of their visit but are moving slow enough to make sure we see them coming. We have maybe a little more than a day before they arrive."

Falke pushed to his feet. He motioned to the guard to join him. "Tell the citizens to stay in the village and out of the forest. I want everyone close to the palace as a safety precaution."

"Zoran will have the dragon armies ready to move," Ualan said. "If General Sten tries anything, he'll have to face all shifters."

"Let's hope it doesn't come to a war," Lyssa said to her husband. "The Federation is powerful. I'm not sure our allies will fly to our rescue."

"I was trying to say before that even though some of the louder voices in the city speak out against shifters, they do not speak for most of us. I believe many would rebel against the Federation for just the promise of being free." Justina never thought of herself as a leader of her people. She never intended to speak on their behalf, but this was a moment in their history, an opportunity to make an alliance with the shifters. She was the only Cysgodian here to witness it.

"Roderic, take your guest someplace she can be comfortable," Kirill said.

"No, wait," Justina protested her dismissal. "I know there had to be shifters who didn't—*don't*—want us here, and still you, the royal families, decided to let us come anyway. We don't judge shifters by those who didn't want to take us in, but we are grateful to you for saving our lives when no one else in the universes would open their planet. Please do not judge Cysgodians by those who say insane things about shifters, and please don't assume that we are not willing to fight."

"Justina," Roderic said softly, trying to take her arm.

The Var king lifted his hand. "It's all right, Roderic."

Justina took a nervous breath. "I mean no disrespect."

"No one is judging you for the shouts of a few," Queen Lyssa said, "nor do we doubt your bravery."

Kirill put his hand over his wife's. "But bravery rarely wins against armed, trained soldiers with droids and cyborgs. One machine could wipe out a quarter of the city before they realized an attack started."

Justina understood their point. "I don't want you to think we are cowards who aren't willing to fight for our freedom."

"No one thinks that," Lyssa assured her.

Justina wished she believed her.

"Roderic," Kirill urged.

Roderic nodded and took her gently by her arm. "Come with me, Justina, please."

She hesitated, wishing she knew the right thing to say to convince them to help free her people. Though their empathy was evident, so was their concern. She couldn't blame them.

Justina let Roderic walk her out of the banquet hall. When they were alone, she said, "I want to thank you for all that you've done for me. Please don't think me ungrateful because of what I said in there. I have to fight for my people. No one else will."

At that, he frowned but didn't answer. He walked a little faster.

Suddenly, he stopped. Roderic released her and faced an empty wall.

"Roderic?" Justina reached for him but stopped when he pressed a series of tiles within the circular pattern on the wall. The tiles didn't move as he touched them, but when he finished, the whole center circle sunk into the wall to reveal a screen.

He glanced at her and pulled a loose strand of her hair from her shoulder. He touched the screen, and a tray slid out. He put the hair inside.

"Siren, meet Justina," Roderic stated.

"Justina recorded, my lord," a computerized voice answered. The machine's tone had a strange quality to it, almost as if it pouted. "Security clearance?"

"Eight," Roderic said.

Siren's tone became firm. "Warning. Cysgodian DNA detected. Would you like me to notify the guards to prepare her for transport to the Federation facility?"

Justina gasped and automatically stepped away from the screen as if she could run from the computer's threat.

"No, Siren," Roderic stated. "Justina is an eight clearance. Override the Cysgodian detection protocol."

"Justina recorded." Siren became pleasant. "Welcome, my lady."

Justina crossed her arms over her chest. She studied Roderic. He wasn't meeting her gaze.

"I said welcome, my lady," Siren repeated, as if irritated.

"Oh, uh, thanks, computer?" Justina muttered.

An image of her standing in the hall came onto the screen. Her brow furrowed and half-open mouth did not make for the most flattering of pictures.

"Thank you, Siren," Roderic pressed a button, and the wall slid over the panel.

"Anything for you, my lord," Siren answered.

"Is she," Justina grimaced, "*with* you?"

"Siren is like that with everyone," Roderic explained. "She's temperamental. I like to think of her as the communications liaison we're not allowed to replace."

The hallway lights flickered.

"I mean, the very talented communications liaison for whom there can be no replacement," Roderic stated louder.

The lights returned to normal.

Was the computer eavesdropping on them?

"Can't you overwrite..." Justina let her words trail off as she glanced up at the ceiling.

"Long before I was born, my Uncle Jarek reprogramed the system and then left to explore space. It was meant to be a prank on his brothers, but by the time he'd returned, he'd forgotten the password he put on Siren's voice actuator. She's been programmed like that ever since," Roderic's voice lifted as if for the computer's hearing rather than hers, "and we're all rather fond of her."

"And what does the eight mean?"

"Eight security clearance means you're a guest." Roderic quickened his pace as they walked down the hall. "You are free to walk around the palace. You can ask Siren for directions or help. Just don't leave the palace. She will notify us if you're taken outside the walls."

Justina hugged her arms over her stomach. Level eight security sounded very much like another form of imprisonment.

12

"PLEASE DON'T THINK ME UNGRATEFUL BECAUSE of what I said in there. I have to fight for my people. No one else will."

Justina's words echoed in Roderic's head. They hurt because it sounded like she didn't trust him to do the honorable thing. More than that, it hurt because he couldn't deny that they had failed the Cysgodians, and she had no reason to trust them.

Shifters told themselves there was a delicate balance between helping the aliens and keeping the Federation from permanent residence—and there was. But there was no delicate balance between right and wrong. What happened to the Cysgodian people was wrong. They had been victims of a biological attack, victims of the Federation's political maneuvering, and now victims of their neighbor's neglect.

The shame became too much to bear.

"It must have been beautiful seeing the country-side from the sky. I'm a little sorry I missed the view when Jaxx flew us." Justina's words were soft. "I forgot to thank him for the rescue."

"I am grateful you were not aware of the ride. It wasn't..." Roderic thought of dangling by one arm in the cold wind and rubbed his wrist. Weakly, he finished, "Pleasant."

Her eyes followed his hand. She stopped walking and pulled at his long sleeve to see his bruised wrist from where Jaxx carried him.

"You need a medical booth," Justina stated. She looked over his body, her eyes sharp as if searching for each detail. "Didn't you get scanned too? I just assumed you were checked."

He put his hand over hers. The feel of her fingers felt better than any medical laser. "It is nothing."

"Siren, where is the medical room?" Justina asked.

"There are several authorized medical rooms in the palace, my lady," Siren answered in a sultry tone. "Do you need me to report a medical emergency?"

"No. Thank you, Siren," Roderic dismissed the computer. "We're all right for now."

"Anything for you, my lord," Siren flirted. The quirky mainframe always amused him but detecting Justina's slight grimace, he saw Siren in a new light.

Siren had been engineered into every room of the palace, even into the center courtyard set aside for the family's private use. She answered questions, tracked life functions, opened doors, prepared food, inventoried weapons, anything they might need. She could even alert the palace guards into action. They depended on her to keep their lives running smoothly.

"Roderic," Justina insisted.

"I will survive a bruised wrist." Roderic glanced around, wondering what else she thought of his home. He'd always been proud of the palace, of his people, of their accomplishments, but after decades of living here, he stopped seeing the fine details. "I hope you don't mind staying in my home. We have guest suites, but alien dignitaries are visiting, and it would be safer..." He paused to correct himself. "I would feel better if you were near so I can protect you."

She nodded. "Wherever you have room for me. As long as there is a place to sit down."

Roderic brought her to the section of the palace where his family kept separate apartments. They passed his parent's door, and he motioned at it, "This is where my mother keeps her lab." They made their way to his door and stopped. He pointed further down the hall. "There is my brother's home." He placed his hand against the scanner to open his door. "And this is us."

Us.

The word sounded more intimate than he intended, but he didn't correct it.

When she stepped past him into the home, Roderic's hand lifted automatically to stop her. He clutched his fist and forced his arm down. Thankfully, she didn't see the gesture.

What would she think, seeing his home? She had so little, just a stack of reading material next to a mat and no furniture.

Justina took a few steps and then stood in the entryway as he shut the door behind them. Her breathing visibly deepened, but she didn't speak. Her head turned as she took in the vast oval space and then tilted back to look at the ceiling.

Roderic thought of the food bag hanging from

FERAL PRINCE

her ceiling and looked up at his to where a large crystal chandelier was suspended beneath a dome of tinted glass. The dangling crystal shards diffused the light, and at times tiny rainbows danced on his walls.

"This is yours?" she asked.

He wanted to answer 'ours' but refrained.

"You have use of everything you see." He made his way to the seating area and stepped around the couch. A long banner with the royal symbol of an upright wild cat hung next to a fireplace. "And everything you don't."

He lifted the banner to reveal a button hidden in the wall. "This will activate the food simulator. Under the best of circumstances, we dine in the banquet hall together, but given what is happening, perhaps it is best we eat here. Use it whenever you wish."

She stared at him.

"If you're cold, the fireplace is activated by voice command, or you can ask Siren to change the temperature." He gestured to the massive fireplace.

She kept staring.

He went to a platform where a yellow curtain trimmed with blue had been suspended from the ceiling in the corner. Drawing the curtain to the side, he revealed a wide bathing tub. The curtains allowed for complete privacy or could be pushed aside for light. "Here is the water bath or," he pointed at the wall to another panel, "a decontaminator if you prefer lasers."

Roderic looked at her expectantly. She stayed in the entryway and merely nodded at him.

He pointed across the room to where his bed was behind another set of yellow and blue curtains. "The bed. The curtains will make it completely dark if you wish."

"I don't like complete darkness," she answered softly.

Roderic remembered that it reminded her of death. He went to the curtains and pulled them open to reveal large silk pillows and a thick cream-colored comforter embroidered with a blue royal cat. "You're welcome to leave them open. The bed is yours. I'll be fine on the couch. Or, if that makes you uncomfortable, I can stay with my brother."

"Please don't leave me alone in here." She swallowed nervously. "There is enough room in here for ten families."

"You don't like it?"

Justina slowly stepped around the couch toward the fireplace. She lifted the banner and pushed the button to reveal the food simulator. The wall panel moved to show the unit, and she dropped the banner to stare at it.

"Do you need me to show you how to use it?" he asked, desperate to please her. "You can have anything you want. As much as you want."

When she turned to look at him by the bed, a tear had slid down her cheek. "It's the most beautiful thing I've ever seen." She turned to touch the edge of the unit lightly. Most visitors looked at the sculptures or artwork, even the carvings along the fireplace and the elegant furnishings. She stared at a food simulator. "Just right here, in the home. No calculating how many bites until the next ration drop." She then went to the bath. "And a bath. Anytime you want, you can be clean. You don't have to decide if you want to drink the water or use it."

Roderic didn't know what to say. An apology for all she had gone through formed on his lips, but even in his head, it sounded like it wasn't enough. Words would be cheap when their actions to help the Cysgodians had fallen short.

"We really do live in different stories, don't we, Prince?" She wiped the tear from her cheek. "Yours is like a daydream in the light. Mine is...'

Justina took a deep breath and stiffened.

"I apologize. I sound ungrateful and like I'm

pitying myself." She turned to the simulator. "Yes, can you please show me how to make water?"

Roderic crossed to the unit and typed in the simple commands, careful to do it slowly so she could learn the sequence. The unit's front door slid open, and he reached in for a blue mug with water in it. It had been programmed to supply dishware to match his home.

"Just like that." She whispered as she sniffed the clear liquid. "Instant water."

Justina took a small drink before gulping down the contents. She studied the mug before handing it back to him. He placed it inside the unit and tapped another button to remove the dish.

Alone, standing close, he thought of the woods. They'd been like this before, eyes locked, bodies gravitating toward each other. He felt her inside him like liquid fire in his blood.

"Will they tell us when the Federation gets here?" she asked.

Roderic nodded.

"What do you think your elders will decide?" Justina didn't step away from him, but neither did she lean closer.

"I know you have no reason to believe this, but we want to help." Roderic wanted to touch her desperately. He wanted her against his chest and in his arms so that he could fold her into himself and protect her from the world. If the time came and it was safe for her to return, he wasn't sure he could keep his promise and bring her back to the city.

"I believe you."

"I'm sorry that we have not done more. You're right not to trust us."

Justina shook her head. "You have a duty to your shifter population as well. You gave us refuge on this planet, and that did stop the virus from killing us. No one blames you..." She took a deep breath. "No one *with reason* blames you for what the Federation does. You did not ask for them on your planet. My people did—at least our government did, and we put them into power. Cysgod joined the Alliance. We invited them into our lives. You have repeatedly told them you don't want them in your lives. It's a complicated mess, isn't it? Without the Federation, we wouldn't have known about this place or had the means to come here. But the price they demand in return is high. They're using us to force you into joining them. Don't do it."

Roderic couldn't control his movements. His fingers lifted to her face, lightly touching the natural discoloration near her temple before gliding over her cheek and along her jawline to her chin. "You are unlike any woman I have ever met, and I have met aliens from all over the universes. To think that you have been here all this time, there in that city, and I only just now found you. I don't want to let you go."

"You know what we feel can't be allowed more than a fleeting moment," Justina said. "If you continue touching me, you have to know we can't be more than this. Never life mates. Not half mates. Not together. If nothing happens and I go back to the city, their Sweeper borgs and drones will be watching everything I do. If I die, I will not have you living the rest of your life alone."

"What if our stories merged? What if things were different?" he asked.

Her words both gave him hope and tore out his heart at the same time. She acknowledged what was between them but also denied its promise.

"The fact that you ask that proves how different our stories are, Prince," she answered.

He knew she used his title to keep him at arm's distance, perhaps reminding herself of the gulf between them or maybe simply reminding him of the same.

"What I feel for you, Justina, you have to know, it's special. It is real." He continued the light caresses against her cheek. His thumb traveled along the bottom edge of her lip. Wisps of her lovely red hair tickled the back of his hand. "I can't pretend it's not. I can't stop it any more than I can stop the beating of my heart or my need for air."

"You're not making this easy." She closed her eyes and turned into his palm.

"Nothing about our lives is easy." He chuckled, though the humor was bittersweet. "Why would falling in love be?"

Love?

Her breath caught, and she stared into his eyes.

He hadn't meant to say it, but he knew he meant it. Married men said it happened like that for shifters. All it took was a single moment, and the animal inside them knew. His moment had come when she stood defiantly over Fiora's unconscious body. He'd been in shifter form, and she'd been throwing sticks at him and yelling at him to leave. His human self hadn't wanted to delve too deeply into the illogic of their situation, so he'd tried to ignore the instinct.

"Tell me not to touch you, my lady, and I will obey." It was his turn to hold his breath as he waited for her answer.

13

JUSTINA TRIED TO DO THE RIGHT THING. BUT what was that? Ending this moment before they became so entangled, they would never be free of the other? Was that right? It didn't feel right.

The touch of his hand, so tender and light, had the power to brand her completely. She watched the light swirl in his gaze, shifting with the animal he could become only to fade once more. The Federation always loomed close, but this time it was different. They followed her here.

With all the talk of fighting and change, she knew the simplest thing that the Var and Draig could do was turn her over with an excuse as to why she was there.

"Tell me not to touch you, my lady, and I will

obey." Roderic's breath caught as he waited for her to answer. His fingers stopped their tiny movements, and his eyes begged.

Her heartbeat quickened. That was one command she couldn't give.

"Touch me," she whispered.

The hand against her cheek became firm as he cupped her face in his palm. The contact shot through her with liquid awareness. His lips parted in invitation as he leaned toward her. When she inhaled, his scent filled each breath.

She mimicked his movement, letting her hand press against his bearded cheek before fingers glided into his hair. The strands felt like silk against her skin. No part of her wanted this to stop.

His eyes flashed again, but the animal side buried within him didn't frighten her. She pulled him into her kiss. The first brush of his mouth exploded against her like the blast from a droid. It sent electric waves over her body until every nerve felt like it was on fire and needed him to put out the flames.

His mouth moved against her, and his tongue skated along her lips. The universes faded away at that moment, disappearing into a dream until Roderic and his touch were the only reality. His kiss lingered, sweet and gentle as if there was nothing else that he would rather be savoring. His velvet tongue slipped into her mouth.

Justina wasn't sure which one of them took the first step toward the bed, but they traveled across the room within the seconds of that kiss. Her knees hit the mattress, startling her enough to break contact.

An animalistic noise sounded in his chest. Her fingers had tousled his hair into framing his passionate eyes. His heavy breath punctuated his words as he whispered, "I want you."

"I want you," she repeated.

He pulled his shirt over his head and threw it behind him, not caring where it landed. She gasped to see bruises not only on his wrist but on his chest and shoulder.

"Do you—?" she began.

"No. They'll heal. It would hurt me more to leave you." He kissed her again. This time she crushed against his naked chest. Heat radiated over the peaks and valleys of his defined muscles. Bare flesh beckoned her touch, and she ran her hand everywhere she could reach—around his neck, down his back, his chest, his waist. When she reached his hips, she slid her fingers into his waistband.

Desire pulsed hard and heavy in her stomach.

She clawed at his pants, not feeling the way to free him of the tight material. Her hand bumped the obvious arousal growing between his thighs.

Roderic tugged at her gown, quickly pulling it over her head. He threw it toward the couch and as the material landed, so too did something breakable. The sound of shattering glass followed by the tinkling of broken shards scattering across the floor caused a smile to cross his features.

She stood only in short boots. Before she could take them off, he had his hands on her waist. He jerked her hips against his, pressing himself into her as his pants blocked their flesh from touching.

Roderic groaned, rocking against her several times. His hands gripped her ass to keep her close. His chest teased her breasts with each sway of their bodies, brushing up against her hard nipples. Her thighs tightened in anticipation.

Roderic turned her back to the bed and pushed her hips, so she dropped onto the embroidered cat. His eyes flashed as he leaned over her. She crawled backward as he came over her. Each movement sent a ripple over his muscles.

Her heart beat faster until she worried it might explode out of her chest.

It was not lost on her that this was the fantasy of

almost every Cysgodian woman—plush surroundings, a royal shifter ready to devour every inch of her.

Roderic drew his mouth to her breast, kissing it deeply before applying the same treatment to the other side only to return. Hands felt as if they roamed everywhere, staking claim.

"Your smell," he groaned against her.

She tensed, worried at the thought of being dirty. It took her a moment to recall she'd been decontaminated.

His lips trailed from her breasts to her stomach. Hands gripped her inner thighs, pushing them open. The short boots grazed over the fine bedding.

He kissed near her navel before licking downward to her sex. She gasped, tensing and pushing up as his mouth sealed itself to her. The tip of his tongue swirled against the tight bud of her center heat. The gentle pressure caused tremors to erupt through her. Warm fingers slid dangerously close to his mouth, dipping between her folds. She waited for that moment he'd enter her but the fingers teased.

Roderic's hand changed course, and he reached for a breast. He tweaked her nipple, and a tiny orgasm released into his intimate kiss. Her feet pushed into the bed, hating the way the boots caught in the material to hamper her movements.

"Roderic," she begged. "Please."

His hand left her breast. He released his mouth and fumbled for his waistband. She closed her eyes, hot and needy, as she arched on the bed.

He came over her with stalking grace. His loosened pants brushed her inner thighs. She rubbed her legs against him, inching his pants down to reveal naked hips. Warm flesh stirred her passions even more.

She'd thought his mouth felt incredible, but it didn't compare to the rub of his arousal along her sex. The thick tip found her ready opening and dipped just enough to tease her more.

"Roderic," she gasped. Her body begged him to end its torment.

His mouth claimed hers just as his body slid deep. They rocked together, moaning and desperate for release.

"Justina," he whispered her name against her mouth, the sound reverent. "Justina."

Her eyes locked with his, transfixed.

Excitement built until finally climax claimed her. She cried out softly under the weight of the pleasure. Seconds later, he joined her in release. Tensing over her as his hips jerked against hers.

He stayed like that, breathless, expression surprised as if he couldn't believe what had happened.

Roderic fell next to her on the bed and smiled as he pulled her next to his chest. "Forget everything else. Let's never leave this bed."

Justina nodded in agreement. That was what she wanted too. It was as she feared. Being with Roderic was more than she could have dreamed possible, and it was also one thing that fate probably wouldn't let her have.

JUSTINA DIDN'T KNOW WHEN SHE'D FALLEN asleep, but she felt safe and warm. The sensation was so foreign that she thought she was stuck in a dream, a wonderfully beautiful dream she never wanted to end. It was the softness beneath her body that first brought her to awareness. Her mat on the floor was unforgiving, and by morning her joints usually ached.

She stirred against the silken mattress, stretching her arms and legs, reaching for Roderic before she opened her eyes. Her hands and feet met with an empty bed.

"Roderic?" she called, wanting him to come back.

Justina stirred again, stretching into different

positions as she tried to convince herself to sit up. She realized her boots were missing. Roderic must have taken them off her.

When he didn't answer, and the home remained silent, she rolled to the side and looked beyond the half-drawn curtain into the empty suite. He wasn't there.

Naked, she walked barefoot through the room, feeling as if at any moment a soldier would burst in and demand to know why she was there before dragging her out by her hair. It wasn't a logical feeling considering she was deep within the Var palace, but more a reflection of the insecurities she felt in being an outsider inside the royal castle.

"Um, Siren?" she asked, uncertain. "Are you watching me right now?"

"Yes, my lady," a cheery Siren answered. "I am monitoring your vitals. You are alive."

"Thanks, Siren." That's not what Justina had meant. She really hoped Siren didn't record everything people did in the palace.

A green dress had been laid across the back of Roderic's couch. She lightly touched the soft material but didn't pick it up. The color was better suited to her.

"I do show elevations consistent with postcoital

hormones." Siren continued.

"What does postcoital mean?" Justina asked.

"You had sex with Prince Roderic," Siren answered. "Would you like me to report these new readings to Princess Tori in her laboratory, so she has a complete medical file?"

"No!" Justina shouted, holding up her hands to the empty room as if she could stop the computer by sheer will. "Please, don't do that. Siren, erase records of my postcoital readings."

"I'm sorry, my lady, you do not have the authority to erase palace records." The computer didn't sound apologetic. "This records interference attempt has been logged and will be routed for review."

"Reviewed by who?" Justina insisted. When the computer didn't answer, she demanded louder, "Siren, reviewed by who?"

"All members of the royal family will receive notice, my lady, as will commanders," Siren answered.

Justina covered her mouth, resisting the urge to argue with the machine. She stood still, stunned and praying the computer mainframe had a sense of humor and would start laughing at any moment.

Siren didn't say anything more.

Justina went to the bathing tub. She thought about trying it but didn't want to waste time if something was happening. She opened her mouth to ask Siren if the Federation had arrived at the palace but then thought better of it. The less she talked to the Var computer, the better. The conversations were not ending well for her.

The free use of a decontaminator was too much to pass up. She pushed the button on the wall, and a panel moved to reveal a decontamination booth. She peeked in before stepping inside. The door slid closed, latching her in the dark booth. For those few seconds in the dark, she held her breath. Cleaning lasers glowed from the sides, hitting the length of her body. She lifted her arms and then tousled her hair to give better access to her scalp as they worked. When it finished, the door opened to let her out.

"Roderic?" she asked as she came from the booth. He still wasn't there.

Justina went to the couch and flipped over the gown before kneeling on the floor. She reached for the bottom hem and pulled the skirt over her head, dragging the dress off the couch as she slid her arms into the armholes and then stood to let it drop over her body. She ignored the cross ties along the side, letting them hang loose.

Next, she went to the food simulator, pushed the buttons Roderic had shown her for water, and took out her mug. She drank it quickly and then returned the mug to the unit. Because she could, and because she didn't know how to ask for anything else, she did it two more times.

She bit her lip and hesitated before asking, "Siren, what is the most popular food people eat from these things and how do you make it?"

"Allow me, my lady."

The unit dinged, and Justina opened the door. Excited, she pulled out a steaming bowl. Giant three-eyed bugs floated with legs pointed upward in a brown sauce.

"What...?" Justina gagged and shoved the bowl back into the unit. She wasn't sure if it was the liquid sloshing in the bowl or if the bugs were alive, but she swore she saw the legs twitch.

"Elteeb Stew is reported to be the most asked for food from simulators in the recorded universe this last star month, made popular by the Torgan Market alien food challenge," Siren said. "Many are playing the daring game."

Justina pushed the button to get rid of the dish.

It was now official. Siren hated her.

15

Roderic sat across from his father and
uncles in the royal office. The room hadn't been
redecorated since he was a child, and he found
comfort in that familiarity. Like the rest of the
palace, the elaborate tile work covered the walls,
hiding access to Siren and other secret compart-
ments. The fireplace was large enough for him to
walk into and graced a gigantic wall. As very young
children, they had camped in front of the fire on the
long woven red and blue rug, all of them shifted and
sleeping in a pile of fur. Uncle Kirill had let them
take turns trying on his crown as they sat at his desk.

His father sat in one of the chairs next to the rug,
and Falke lounged in the other. The king leaned

MICHELLE M. PILLOW

against the front of his stone desk with his arms crossed. There were empty chairs and a couch nearby, but Roderic was left standing before the barren fireplace like a child about to be punished.

Roderic had not wanted to leave Justina alone, but he'd been summoned to the king's office to tell them everything that had been going on in Shelter City. Since the shifters weren't supposed to be near that area without permission, he wasn't surprised that they had questions now that he's shown up with one of the citizens.

He was surprised, however, by how much they already knew.

"You might as well tell all. We know about the food simulators. I don't know why you children think you can fool us. We're your parents," his father said, shaking his head. "Any mischief you can think of we've already done."

"So you know that we...?" Roderic looked at his hands.

"Of course, the crew is not going to come to Qurilixen without seeing Samantha," Falke said with a laugh. "She was their captain for years before we married. She gave them that ship they're flying."

"We knew about you and Jaxx. He's being questioned by his family just as you are now," Kirill said. "Who else helped you?"

Roderic's cousin Payton had been involved, but he wasn't about to drag her into trouble with them.

"Right," Falke said at his silence. "Payton too."

"I didn't..." Roderic protested.

"You didn't have to," Falke muttered before leaning his head against his fist. "I know my daughter."

"If there is to be punishment, I take full responsibility," Roderic said. "But I will not apologize for trying to help."

"And we won't apologize for not stopping you," Kirill answered with a wry smile.

"We knew it was only a matter of time before you children did something," his father said. "And while everyone is watching and reporting on our actions..." He waved dismissively.

"Jaxx was right," Roderic muttered. "It's the camping thing all over again."

"Camping thing?" Kirill asked.

"When we snuck off as children and camped in the woods," Roderic explained.

All three men laughed and nodded as if sharing their private joke.

"They thought they were stealthy." His father shook his head, laughing harder.

"I was afraid none of them would graduate from their war training," Falke added. "What an embarrassment that would have been—royal shifters who couldn't master basic evasion techniques. The guards had to pretend not to see you crawling through the shadows even though half the time you were upwind."

"And the stories you came up with whenever you started to get caught," Kirill added, wiping his eye as a tear of amusement formed in the corner.

"My favorite was when you said you went out early to check the palace walls for mold growth because you were all simply fascinated by your mother's work." His father laughed harder. "Your mother sent you out with specimen kits, and you spent the next fortnight cataloging mud samples, and you had to pretend to be riveted by the lessons."

Roderic grimaced as they laughed harder.

"But we digress," Kirill stated, pushing up from where he leaned against his desk. "We're here to talk about the Federation. Is there anything else you need to tell us? What threats are there in the city that we haven't heard about?"

There was no point in trying to lie about it. They already knew who was involved.

"Fiora predicted an explosion of an old still someone had put in an alleyway. It would have been an accident caused by someone who didn't understand the technology. It's been stopped, but Jaxx and I did see marsh farmers dragging old still equipment in the direction of the city. We might want to do forest sweeps and confiscate any old equipment, so we don't have a repeat," Roderic said.

Kirill nodded. "Falke."

"I'll see to it," Falke answered.

"We've also run across some men from the city out in the woods. They go by the names Raimon, Partha, Bharath, and X. We think they're the ones trading with the marsh farmers," Roderic added. "They're angry, but we can't blame them. Their families are being mistreated, and they're helpless to provide better."

His elders nodded in agreement.

"There's Doyen. Jaxx and Payton thought they'd killed him, but he's a tough one. Details are unclear, but from what we can tell, he crawled out of a grave and found a handheld medic. We think he stays in the city, but he's been building a following. We're keeping an eye on him. He's a fanatical blood

MICHELLE M. PILLOW

preacher who touts sacrificing shifters and drinking our blood to promote a long life—as if they can absorb our longevity and vitality from the blue radiation into themselves. He's a charlatan but charismatic. People are listening. He is a concern."

"I hesitate to ask if there is anything else," Kirill said.

"We have a contact in the city." Roderic was unable to meet Falke's gaze. "Yevgen. He's a cyborg. Somehow, he manages to stay hidden from Federation detection, but he seems to know everything going on in the city. He's helped us on several occasions. He is the reason we found out Fiora was imprisoned. He helped shelter Fiora and Jaxx. And he alerted us to Doyen."

"When you go to the city to retrieve Starrs or take Justina back, whichever happens first, you will go to this Yevgen and invite him to the palace," Kirill ordered.

Roderic frowned. "He won't want to come."

"Insist," Falke stated. "If he has intel, we need it."

"He definitely won't come if *I* ask," Roderic explained.

"Then who?" Kirill walked around his desk and took a seat.

"He appears to have developed a soft spot for," Roderic glanced at Falke and scrunched up his face, "Payton. He was very interested to know what she thinks of the idea of half mate—"

"No." Falke dropped his hand from his face and his arm hit against the side of the chair with a heavy thud. "Under no circumstance is my daughter to half mate. If she is meant to marry a cyborg, so be it, but she will be treated as a wife and should be loved above all others."

"I don't think Payton returns his sentiments." Roderic hoped to calm his uncle. "And he seems more machine than human, so I'm not sure how much he really can feel beyond vague curiosity and remanent emotions."

"I don't care if they're inclinations or full-blown emotions, I'm not allowing my daughter to subject herself to a life without—"

"Falke," Kirill interrupted his brother. "You cannot lock your daughter in the palace. Do not make rash declarations and force me to overrule you as king."

"You have sons. You cannot possibly understand," Falke dismissed.

Roderic felt sorry for Payton. Out of all the men in that generation, she was born to the Var military's commander prince. He'd spent half his life forced into the war King Attor started and often talked like he was commanding an army into battle.

Kirill touched the console built into the top of his desk. A soft glow illuminated his face. He pushed a few buttons. His mouth quirked a little at the side. "We have an internal interference report coming from your section of the palace, Quinn."

"Is Tori...?" His father stood and made a move as if he'd run to his wife.

Kirill lifted his hand and tried not to laugh. "Not Tori. Apparently, our Cysgodian guest has tried to delete some of Siren's records."

Quinn changed directions and came around the desk. Falke stood to join them. Roderic watched their serious expressions. What had Justina done?

The urge to protect her filled him, and he took an unconscious step toward the office door.

Kirill looked at him with an arched brow. His father glanced at him and then back down at the desk. Suddenly, Falke began to laugh, tossing his head back and slapping the flat of his hand against the desk.

"Something you want to tell us?" Kirill tried and failed to keep an even expression.

"I suppose it is about time we had," his father

chuckled, struggling to finish, "a talk about how to," he laughed harder, "please a woman so she's not embarrassed about..."

Falke laughed louder.

"What?" Roderic demanded, crossing his arms over his chest.

Kirill motioned to the desk and stepped back to make room so Roderic could read for himself. Siren had sent an alert to the entire royal family and a few of the top palace guards warning that Justina had tried to initiate the deletion of the record of her postcoital hormones after sex with Roderic.

Falke slapped him on the back, still laughing.

"I'd offer to delete it, but it's out there," Kirill said. "Luckily, no one from the palace will share this failed liaison with any visitors."

"I didn't fail," Roderic protested. He was reasonably certain Justina had been well pleased by him. He also didn't want to discuss it with his father and uncles.

They laughed harder.

"There's more to report," Roderic put forth, trying to change the subject.

The statement sobered them up some. Falke nodded and returned to his chair. Kirill sat at his desk. His father crossed his arms and remained by the king.

Roderic took a deep breath. Their attention turned fully to him. Their lingering smiles fell.

"This might be a serious problem," Roderic stated. "A man we call Yellow Shirt, because of a distinct shirt he is never without, found one of the food simulator caches before we could set them up in the forest. We're waiting on the fuel cells. Yevgen is the reason we know who took them. He got a glimpse of the man with one of the units. Jaxx and Fiora went so she could get a clear read on his timeline. Before Jaxx was attacked by petty thieves, Fiora had a vision of Yellow Shirt giving the unit to one of the military guys in exchange for a bag. We do not know what is in the bag, but it can be assumed it was payment for the information."

His father closed his eyes and leaned his head back to look at the ceiling with a deep sigh. Falke leaned against his fisted hand, his lips tightening. Kirill paused what he was doing on his desktop.

"So they know what's been done," Kirill stated. "Very well."

"Is there anything else?" Falke asked.

Roderic shook his head. There were plenty more stories from the city about its corruption and problems, but nothing that would change their current course.

"We continue as planned," Kirill said. "Hopefully, Princess Fiora will have a vision that might help us, but we cannot expect her to see everything with as much pain as the visions can cause her. She's agreed to stay in the palace, but Jaxx does not want her anywhere near the general. We won't give him a chance to recapture her."

Having predictions of the future would have been helpful. There would be a lot of strangers in the palace, but the shifters refused to treat Fiora like General Sten had during her imprisonment. He'd made her perform readings for the entertainment of his guests, drugging her to make the visions stronger. It had amounted to torture.

"Has the Federation made contact?" Roderic asked.

"The convoy we spotted in the forest is on its way here. After General Sten marched his army on the Draig palace and was humiliated, he's taking a more tactful approach. They wish to meet today. Since Tori and Nadja have not finished analyzing the vial you brought, we're looking at ways to distract the general into giving them more time. Samantha has suggested we entertain the Nenarraten and Shandrot ambassadors while they're here. Plus, we have the visiting Draig royals. There will be a formal banquet. General Sten will not make demands with intergalactic witnesses. It should buy us time. Since the ambassadors were already here, they can't accuse us of avoiding the conversation."

"Your brother and I will be busy at the banquet making sure our off-world guests are too entertained to retire to their suites," his father added. "I depend on you to help your mother. Watch over her and get her out of the palace if the Federation decides to act."

Roderic nodded that he would.

"I've ordered some of the men to take the village children on a survival camping trip to the shadowed marshes so as not to alarm them when the Federation arrived. They'll be safe there," Falke added. "They left this morning."

"Falke, I'm sure you have much to do. Quinn, can you and Samantha prepare the servants for tonight? Lyssa is trying to make contact with some of her old associates from her HIA days." Kirill stood. "I'm going to meet with Ualan and go over our options. What happens today will change the course for all shifters. We must tread carefully and show a firm shifter alliance. We might not want to relive the wars, but the Myrddinians won't hesitate to use this to stoke discontent between the Draig, Var, and the Federation. They would love nothing more than to start a war on all fronts."

The Myrddinians were a faction of shifter purists named after the sadist Lord Myrddin, who served as an advisor to Roderic's grandfather, King Attor. As much of a concern as they would usually cause, sadly, too much was happening to give them much thought.

Roderic slipped out of the royal offices while Kirill finished giving them directions. He shut the door quietly behind him and turned to go home to Justina. He needed to make sure she was not upset about their night together.

"So, did you give me up to save yourself?"

Roderic glanced to where Payton stood, arms crossed, as she leaned against the wall waiting for him. She was not dressed for royal visitors but rather for an adventure in the forest. Pants with cross-laces up the side of each leg matched the leather shirt with laces down the front. Both made for easy removal before a shift. Her dark hair had been piled on the top of her head.

"They already knew," he stated.

She pushed away from the wall to join him as he

walked toward his home. "So, how much trouble are we in this time?"

"More than usual," he answered. "But not for the reason you think."

"Oh?"

Roderic told her a short version of what happened with Justina, Jaxx, and Fiora before finishing, "You should probably cancel whatever plans you had and prepare for the banquet tonight."

"Good idea. It sounds like this is where all the action is going to be anyway." Payton slowed her step.

Roderic quickened his pace, thinking only of reaching Justina.

"Oh, and Roderic," she called after him.

Roderic turned to look at her.

Payton grinned. "If you need any help on how the female body works, let me know. We are complicated creatures."

He grimaced. Damn Siren and her all-royal security alerts.

Roderic flung his hand toward her in dismissal. "I am not discussing sex tips with you, Payton, or any of the cousins."

As he strode away from her, she yelled, "No need to be embarrassed. Your prudishness about asking for help is probably why you're not any good at it!"

Roderic heard the royal office door open. He chuckled at the sound of Payton's running feet as she avoided her father.

16

Justina was not home when he returned. The clothes he'd laid out for her were gone. Panic set in at the idea of her leaving without telling him. Had she gone to intercede with the Federation before they arrived? What would General Sten do to her? Or had she run away from him because she was ashamed about what happened between them? Was she angry that he'd left without waking her? He had debated, but she looked so peaceful sleeping he couldn't disturb her.

Then he remembered the level eight security. That meant she must have still been in the palace.

"Siren, where is Justina?" Roderic demanded.

"She is in the southwest guard tower, my lord," the computer answered.

Roderic left the apartment, rushing through the halls toward the southwest tower. What was she doing up there?

The southwest tower was one of four square towers built along the top of the palace. They were part of the oldest section. Before the comfort features of the palace had been updated, the old chimneys used to filter up through them to ventilate smoke. Sky bridges had been built between them to create open walkways high above the ground.

As Roderic climbed the enclosed tower stairs, he let a half shift take over his body. Still upright, his muscles became stronger and more agile. He took the steps four at a time, winding his way to the top. A cool breeze met him as he neared the top. Instantly, he detected her scent.

As he came through the open door, he saw Justina turn to greet him. Her eyes widened in shock, and she stumbled back against the tower opening. Roderic darted forward to grab her hand to keep her from falling over the side. A slight growl left his throat. Seeing his fur-covered fingers gripping her arm, he pushed all traces of the animal back inside.

"It's me," he said.

Justina gave a relieved laugh. "You startled me. I wasn't expecting that."

"What are you doing up here?" He joined her near the edge.

"I'm not sure. I guess I wanted to see what the planet looked like from your view." Justina didn't look at the view, though. She stared at him. "I thought maybe I could see where the Federation was from here, but I can't."

Roderic pointed to the northwest. "You're facing the wrong direction. They're that way."

"Oh." She stepped out of the covered section of the tower onto one of the sky bridges to look.

Lights shone from the roof below, dissipating into the expanse of green-blue overhead. Roderic saw two guards halfway between the towers. They must have moved when Justina came up the stairs to give her distance. He lifted his hand in greeting and they nodded in return.

"I still don't see anything," she said.

Roderic narrowed his gaze and searched the distant sea of trees. "There's too much coverage."

Banners which were anchored lower on the towers flapped wildly in the stiff breeze. He had seen them many times, the image of an enormous golden cat boldly displayed against a blue background. The wind whipped her hair, and he motioned that she should return to the enclosure.

"I tried to walk across, but my knees started shaking," she admitted. "I almost crawled through behind the walls to keep the wind from pushing me over, but those men were blocking the way and staring at me. I'm sure they'd find it amusing for a grown woman to crawl like a child."

"I don't think they're staring because they find you amusing." Roderic pushed a wild strand of red hair away from her cheek. She hadn't tightened the cross-laces of her dress, and the material hung loosely over her body. When the wind blew against her, it gave teasing peeks of her curves.

Roderic couldn't look away. His body stirred to be near her.

"I have to tell you something," Justina said.

He stiffened in worry.

"I made a mistake. It felt weird knowing Siren was in the room with me, so I wanted to make sure I wasn't being recorded by her. There was a miscommunication. She wanted to send my vital signs to your mother and said something about the fact we'd been together, and I thought that would surely make things worse for everyone, considering the Federation is coming for me. Plus, it's your mother.

So I told her no and asked her to delete the fact we had sex, but she, uh..." Justina pressed her lips together.

"Sent the information to my entire family and a few of the commanders," he finished for her.

Justina's brow furrowed and she groaned. "So you know?"

Roderic nodded.

"So, everyone knows?" She pressed her hand to her forehead.

"Does that worry you?"

She dropped her hand. "Only if it causes problems for you."

He thought of his family's teasing. It would be a long time before they let that joke go. "No. No problems for me. I am not ashamed to be with you."

He looked at her mouth, desperately wanting to kiss her.

"Good." She seemed to relax.

This was not the time for sexual thoughts. The palace was full of visitors. The Federation was literally at their doorstep. Lives depended on what happened today. In no reality could he see the general allowing her to stay with him without demanding a price in return. Nor would they allow him to live with her in Shelter City.

"After you rescued her, Fiora gave me a prediction."

"Did she?" Justina closed the distance between them and touched his arm. "Was it about Shelter City?"

Roderic put his hand over her chilled fingers. "She told me that my timeline has so much pain and heartache in it that she didn't want to tell me about it."

"Oh." Her eyes turned downward. "Maybe she's wrong. You said she wasn't doing well with the visions."

"I think she must have meant what I'm feeling now," Roderic said.

"Heartache?"

"Fear," he stated. "And yes, heartache. Heartache at the idea of sending you back to Shelter City. Heartache at the thought of you being at the mercy of General Sten. Heartache at the thought of begging you to leave this planet with me and never coming back to be with my family. Heartache at the thought of not being able to spend every minute with you. I don't want to be without you, Justina."

A tear slid down her cheek. "I'm sorry. I should have been stronger. I should have resisted how I felt about you, but..."

"But you could no sooner stop breathing than stop feeling what we feel," he finished. "It's the same for me."

Justina lifted up on her toes to kiss him. Her mouth was cold from the wind. His hands found hold on her hips as he pulled her into a corner of the tower that couldn't be seen from either walkway. Her breath caught as their lips separated. He trapped her against the stone, trying to block the wind. Desperation fueled the air between them. They might not have many more of these moments together.

Her hands moved down his body to pull at his pants. She fumbled with his waistband. "Where is the tie?"

"Let me." Roderic unfastened his pants, as eager to join as she. Their night together had not tempered his desire. If anything, it made the need worse.

Justina lifted her skirt, exposing the length of her legs. It was all the invitation he needed. Roderic swept his foot against the inside of her boot, sliding her legs open.

Roderic kissed her deeply as he lifted her from the ground. He held her hips and pressed her against the wall. They came together in a shared frenzy of raw emotion.

Their lips slid apart, and they breathed heavily into each other as a primal rhythm took over. The stout wind at his back seemed to push him deeper into her. When their climax hit in perfect unison, it was as wild as their lovemaking had been.

Roderic eased her onto her feet. His forehead rested against hers as he gazed down at the press of their bodies, the seductive view of clothing and limbs tangled together.

"Run away with me," he whispered. "Into the high skies. We'll take Starrs with us and never come back."

She cupped his cheek. "You know that is not an option. You wouldn't be happy in space, and I wouldn't be happy running away and leaving both our people with a mess to clean up."

"We'd be together," he insisted, even as he knew she was right.

"At what cost?" She shook her head. "Whatever happens, we'll fight. We won't give up. Not on our people. Not on saving them. Not on finding a way to rid ourselves of the Federation. Two people don't matter when hundreds of thousands of lives are on the line."

"I love you," he said, holding her face so that he

may press light kisses to her mouth. "If there isn't time later for me to say it, know I love you."

"And I love you." A tear slid down her cheek to wet his thumb as he held her. "Fiora was right. This is heartache."

17

JUSTINA HAD NOT INTENDED FOR HER FEELINGS
to become so complicated. Perhaps the feelings were
not complex so much as they were real. It was the
situation that was complicated. For the first time in
her life, she knew what she wanted for herself. Not
for her people. Not for Starrs. But for her. She
wanted Roderic. That was it. She wanted a life
with him.

The universes were not fair. Why let her meet
Roderic? Why tempt her heart only to take him
away? It was as she first told him. They were written
in two very different books.

As they'd walked down the steps of the square
tower, she had a sinking feeling that this might be
their last time alone together. The Federation was

coming. If it came down to it, she would have to go with them to stop any conflict that might arise from her leaving. When she'd agreed to come to the palace, it was meant to be in secret. Now she realized it should have occurred to her that they would have put a tracker on her.

For a moment, she let herself wonder what it would take for her to be with Roderic. The Federation would have to release her. His family would have to approve, and the idea of shifters accepting her into their royal family seemed like a long shot. They were friendly people, but she was not royalty. She had grown up on the dirty streets of a city the universes had chosen to forget.

"There you are." Princess Tori came down the hall toward them.

Her hand slipped from Roderic's as they faced his mother.

"Justina, we need more blood samples from you." Tori appeared distracted, as if she had multiple things on her mind at once. Dark circles had formed under her eyes, giving away that she was exhausted. Had the scientist princesses been working all night? "We need you to come to the lab."

"What have you discovered so far?" Roderic asked.

"The food ration you brought does seem to have come from a food simulator," Tori said, "but we're unable to find the same recipe in our database. We will keep looking. However, this proves the Federation is using food simulators to provide rations to Shelter City. Their claim of radiation harm does not seem likely."

"So we're not hurting the Cysgodians if we bring them food?" Roderic insisted.

"I don't believe so. I do know that malnourishment is harming them." Tori frowned. "But making a recommendation as a scientist is far from providing empirical proof of General Sten's neglect. Until we figure out what the altered recipe is and how it affects Cysgodian biology, my professional recommendation is the best I can do."

"Thank you," Justina said. "It's a start. This means we can set up supply lines to smuggle food into the city." She frowned and took a deep breath. "Or, rather, it means that *someone* can set up supply lines. I wish we would've had this information a week ago. I would still be in the city and not under suspicion. Now I'm not sure how much I'll be able to help."

"Fiora's vision of Yellow Shirt giving one of the simulators to a soldier might make all smuggling impossible. The more I consider the circumstances, it is too much to hope that the man didn't report it to the general," Roderic said.

"This is a nightmare." Tori ran her fingers through her hair and suppressed a yawn. "Come with me, Justina. We need to get back to the lab. Roderic, can you please check with your Aunt Lyssa and see if she has had any luck contacting her friends? See if she can request a database of Cysgodian recipe codes for the food simulator. Perhaps the mystery compound will be revealed as something native to Cysgod. An herb or vegetable product, maybe?"

"The food we are given here does not remind me of the flavors from our homeworld," Justina said. "It never has."

"Have Lyssa send me anything she can get regarding U-194—*no!*—U-196-v classification compounds," Tori said.

"U-196-v," Roderic repeated.

"Yes, good." Tori nodded.

"What are those?" Justina asked.

"They're known to cause masses like the ones we found in you," Tori said.

"Are you saying that the Federation gave me

something that made me sick?" Justina wrapped her arms around her stomach.

Roderic placed his arm over her shoulders and pulled her close to him.

Tori eyed their half embrace but said nothing.

"You're cured now," Roderic said. "We'll make sure you stay that way. Right?"

Tori nodded. "We'll do everything we can, but for now, we need your blood. And we don't know if it was something the Federation gave you or something you ran into while living here that reacted with Cysgodian biology. We are testing all possibilities."

"I'll come back for you, Justina, as soon as I can." Roderic kissed her cheek before running down the hall.

Tori walked quickly, not looking to make sure Justina followed her. She ran her hand over her home scanner and paused just long enough for the doors to open before rushing inside.

Quinn and Tori's home had a distinctly different style than Roderic's in that it wasn't one large open space. Long pillows had been placed on the floor near a low, wide couch on a raised platform in the center of the room by a fireplace. A wall of thick glass obscured whatever was on the other side. As they walked through the home, she saw a room with a long dining table that had enough chairs to host a dozen people.

Justina's entire house would have fit inside the fireplace.

"I need to apologize for the security report earlier," Justina said.

"What security report?" Tori asked, glancing back. "My laboratory is through here."

"It's nothing," Justina dismissed, not going to explain if she had been saved from that embarrassment.

"Are you squeamish?" Tori led her down a hall and then to a metal security door. She placed her hand on a scanner and then opened her eyes wide for a second scan. "We can go to a medical booth if you need to, but it will be much easier and faster if we can just take the blood directly from your arm. I don't know how much we are going to need."

"Do what you need to," Justina said.

The metal door slid open, only to seal them inside once they stepped in.

"You found her," Nadja appeared from behind a large machine. Flashes of light reflected on her face. "Tori, look at the latest results and give me your opinion."

Glass walls encased extended shelves. Bottles of all shapes, sizes, and colors were arranged in a way that would have meaning to whoever understood them. To Justina, they were a mismatch of neatly organized chaos, clean and evenly spaced. Next to the bottles were jars and vials, a wooden box, stone bowls, and empty containers.

Tori took over what Nadja had been doing. "This is from the vial?"

"Yes," Nadja answered. To Justina, she inquired, "You're not squeamish, are you?"

"No." Justina shook her head in denial.

"Sit." Nadja pointed at a chair.

"The closest chemical match is a health supplement for humanoids," Tori said. "The Federation is trying secretly to dose citizens with a health supplement?"

Justina sat in the chair. The curve of the seat bottom caused her to slide all the way back. "Are you talking about the vial with the black liquid?"

"Yes," Nadja answered. She held her arm straight as a demonstration and told Justina, "Lay it flat."

"Why would something healthy need to be a secret?" Justina mimicked the movement and stretch her arm along the arm of the chair.

"Palm down," Nadja said.

Justina turned her hand. A strap wound around her wrist, and the chair arm moved to lift her hand higher. A panel raised to cover the inside of her elbow. Green lights glowed softly from underneath.

"I want to know why the instructions were to only give a single drop to the most aggressive citizens." Tori stood and crossed to one of the shelves. She slid the glass aside and pulled out the vial of black liquid. "I'm rerunning it."

"I ran it twice," Nadja stated. To Justina, she instructed, "And a poke."

A sharp prick hit the inside of her elbow. Justina jumped a little in surprise. Her blood flowed down a tube from behind the elbow panel. The dark red contrasted the clean white of the chair. She watched it wind around where it gathered in a collection jar.

Nadja joined Tori, and they both stared at the screen. "We need to find out what that slight alteration from the health drink is. If you can isolate that—"

"We'll have our answer," Tori finished.

Justina tried to lift up in her chair to watch them but could only hold the position for a few seconds before sliding back.

"Is it the same alteration showing up in the food ration?" Tori asked.

"No, different," Nadja answered.

Justina watched the jar fill, wondering if her blood would spill over once it reached the top. "I think it's done."

Nadja took the jar and replaced it with an empty one. Justina's blood began to fill the second container. "This machine is ancient, but sometimes the old ways are the best. It's faster and gives a clean sample."

"I feel lightheaded." Justina rested her head back.

"Close your eyes and relax," Nadja instructed as she switched out the container for a third.

Justina's eyes drifted shut.

"The general is refusing to go to the banquet and is demanding to see her."

Justina gasped and opened her eyes at the gruff male voice. She sat up in the chair. Her arm was no longer trapped in the blood device. She searched the laboratory for Roderic, but he wasn't there. Nadja and Tori stood near the two shifter queens and King Kirill.

"He's threatening to report the kidnapping of a

Federation citizen to the Command Center," Kirill continued. "It's an intergalactic offense."

"According to the agreement, he is within his rights to ask for her safe return," Queen Rigan said. "I've been re-reading the documents since we've arrived here and found out what was happening. If we don't return her, they can retaliate and start taking our people to demand prisoner trades. We will be in the wrong."

"We're giving her sanctuary," Tori protested. "My son saved her life. We owe her a life debt."

No one spoke. Justina stood to face them. Rigan glanced apologetically in her direction. No one else could meet her gaze.

"When it was your son and nephew, you stood up to the general," Tori continued. "Kirill, we can't let him take her. I see the way my son looks at her. She's his... She may very well be his life mate. What if it was Korbin or Cason?"

"Salena and Fiora were wrongfully imprisoned by the Federation and brought here in secret. General Sten had to relinquish claim because he'd not followed the agreement," Rigan explained the difference. "Justina is one of theirs. Now it is we who are not following the agreement if we keep her. I'm not saying we hand her over. I'm just saying the consequences we face when we refuse. The dragons are ready to fight those space cadets to the death."

Justina rubbed at her arm where they'd taken the blood. It had healed.

"Are you life mated to Roderic?" Kirill asked.

Justina blinked in surprise at the direct question. She shook her head. "We knew it wouldn't be prudent given the circumstances. If fate..." She took a deep breath, forcing her eyes to remain dry when all she wanted to do was scream and hit things. "I don't want him to be forever alone because we can't be together."

"What assurance will we have that they won't hurt her if she does go back?" Nadja asked. "Have they said?"

"We'd make it clear that we intend to do wellness checks being as Justina has been in our medical care," Queen Lyssa said. "Regardless of how she came to be here, both HIA and ESC humanitarian regulations give us the right for continued medical care as long as Justina wants it. They'll have to comply. At least for the time being."

"Stall him. That's still our best plan. Let's stick to that," Nadja said. "Make him go to the formal banquet. We need more time. We can't hurry the science."

"Lock him out of the palace if you have to," Tori suggested. "He can't prove she's in here. We took out the tracker."

"I agree," Lyssa said. "We have to try—"

"May I speak?" Justina tried to keep calm as they all turned their attention to her. "Do you have enough samples from me to run your tests?"

"Yes," Nadja answered. "We should. Maybe a few hair strands to look for toxin exposures."

Justina yanked several strands of hair out of her head and gave them to Nadja. "There. Now you don't need me here for your science. You have the rations, the vial, and my blood. There is no reason for you to risk a fight with General Sten or, worse, intergalactic sanctions. After the HIA and ESC are involved on that level, anything you find will be tainted by the blow to your reputation. They may even side with the Federation. However, if I go back to Shelter City, we'll all live to fight another day."

"Roderic will never agree," Tori said.

"This isn't his decision to make," Justina answered, "but I'm assuming it may be mine?"

Kirill nodded. "It is your life. Your wishes will be taken into consideration."

"Then take me to General Sten before he sets one foot in this palace. He'll have no reason to stay."

Justina looked at her dress. The clean green material reminded her of how much she didn't belong. This palace was not her home.

"I don't like this," Tori said.

Nadja gently touched her arm, rubbing it. "Eat something before you leave. I promise you that we will not stop working until we have answers."

Justina nodded.

"I'll get Roderic," Lyssa made a move to leave. "He's in the communications tower as the royal ambassador waiting on the HIA response for the official compound requests."

"No. Please." Justina shook her head. "If I see him, I..." She wiped her eyes as a tear slipped by her attempts to be strong. "He'll try to stop me, and I might let him. Just tell him he knows how I feel. And that I need to check on Starrs. He'll understand."

Fiora's prediction had been correct. Heartache. All she felt right now was heartache.

18

Roderic felt the world shift underneath him, even as he stood perfectly still. His heart began to beat faster. Something wasn't right. He felt light-headed. He looked at the vents of the communications tower, wondering if something had happened to the air.

"Do you...?" He glanced around the circular room to see everyone still working at their consoles. No one else seemed to notice the change.

Tarc looked up from the communications panel. "My prince?"

Something wasn't right. He felt it deep inside.

"Have Siren find me if they call back before Queen Lyssa returns." Roderic hurried to the lift

MICHELLE M. PILLOW

that would take him from the top of the tower to the ground.

When he was alone in the lift, he pressed his forehead to the wall and took several breaths. Deep panic filled him, causing his hands to shake. The doors opened to let him out, and he pushed past a group of men waiting to go up. He mumbled an apology.

"Roderic!" Fiora ran down the palace hall toward him. Jaxx was several paces behind her. "You have to stop her. You have to stop Justina!"

Roderic skidded to a stop and changed directions to head toward his parents' home.

"No. She's not there. She's..." Fiora held her head in her hands and closed her eyes. "She's heading outside. Not the main gate. Side entrance. Narrow door. Trees. Cat head with open mouth carving."

The entrance she spoke of was on the other side of the palace and rarely used.

"I have her on level eight security. Falke has all the doors locked down. They won't let her out." Roderic tried to breathe a sigh of relief.

Fiora looked horrified as she shook her head. "She's not. They're not. They're wrong."

The half shift rippled over Roderic's body as he

ran past Fiora through the maze of palace halls. He zoomed past two Shandrot men coming out of a corridor, causing them to jump back in alarm in a flurry of feathery pink clothing. Roderic ran faster.

How was this happening? Justina was supposed to be safe in his mother's laboratory. They wouldn't let her out of the palace without telling him. None of this made sense.

Queen Lyssa had gotten summoned to her husband and asked Roderic to wait in the communications tower for a response from her HIA connection while she went to greet Nenarratens so they wouldn't be insulted by her absence. Otherwise, Roderic would have been with Justina in the laboratory.

As he rounded a corner, he saw his family gathered in the hall. Lyssa's guilty eyes met his, and he knew at that moment she'd tricked him. She lifted her hands and began to speak, but he couldn't hear her from the blood rushing through his ears.

His mother pulled Lyssa out of his way. Queen Rigan pressed back against the opposite wall with Nadja. He surged past the women.

At the end of the corridor, blocked by his uncles and King Ualan, he caught a glimpse of Justina's green skirt as she exited the palace.

Roderic growled and braced his shoulder, intent on barreling through to get to Justina.

Falke appeared in front of him, his face shifting as he shoved his hands into Roderic's shoulders to stop him. Under the reversed momentum, Roderic flew back the way he'd come, landing on his ass on the hard floor before flipping over to perch on his hands and feet. His uncle's great strength and centuries of training were no match for Roderic's determination to reach Justina. He tucked his head and charged.

"Roderic!" his mother shouted. He didn't know if she meant to help him or stop him by calling his name.

Roderic slammed his shoulder low into Falke's stomach, sending the commander up and over his body. The sound of Falke landing on King Ualan created chaos behind him. He pushed through to the door.

"Roderic, stop!" Kirill shouted.

"We can explain," Lyssa insisted.

The two guards on either side of the door looked hesitant to stop him from leaving, and he used that moment of uncertainty. He darted past them and came to a stop when faced with an army. He searched for Justina in the crowd.

Three dozen uniformed Federation soldiers formed a protective barrier around General Sten. Sever stood next to the general, arms crossed as he barely contained his anger. This was not a diplomatic visit, and they made no attempt to hide their weapons or their willingness to use them. A few of the soldiers held blasters, the tips pointed toward the ground but their stance ready to fire. Three armed drones flew above their heads. Four land crafts floated behind the group, with more soldiers standing onboard.

Roderic found her green dress heading into the black horde. "Jus—"

A hand clamped over his mouth. Kirill and Falke grabbed his arms from behind to restrain him.

"It's done," Falke whispered gruffly, as he pulled Roderic back. To a guard, he ordered, "Help us."

A guard wrapped his arms around Roderic's chest and neck, careful not to choke him.

"It's what she wanted," Kirill insisted. "Don't make it worse. We'll explain everything."

Roderic fought them as he focused all his senses on Justina.

"I would like to apologize for any inconvenience that I may have caused, General Sten," Justina said, her voice meek. "It was not my—"

Two soldiers grabbed Justina by her arms. She jerked in surprise at the sudden contact.

"Cysgodian Justina," General Sten stated, his voice booming over his men. "By order of the Federation, we are placing you under arrest for numerous incidences of public disruption, interference with an official census, damage to census drones, theft of scientific food stores for testing purposes, attempted distribution of unsanctioned food, theft of medical property, and attempted treason."

"What...?" Justina struggled in confusion. The guards held her wrists and Sever shackled them with electronic cuffs. "No!"

Roderic bit the hand over his mouth. Kirill swore and jerked his hand away.

"Justina!" Roderic thrust violently against his uncles' restraint. He kicked his legs and lost his balance. The weight of the guard behind him brought him lower to the ground. "*Justina!*"

At the sound of his voice, she thrust her hands up to fight her way free. Her eyes turned to meet his and that brief second burned through him like fiery exhaust from a launching spaceship.

"Restrain the prisoner," General Sten ordered.

"This is not what we agreed!" Queen Lyssa ran from behind them.

Justina waved her cuffed hands, trying to propel her body toward Roderic. Sever grabbed hold of her cuffs with one hand and swung the fist of his other. He struck Justina with the back of his hand, half slap, half punch, and sent her twirling into the arms of nearby soldiers.

Roderic roared with pure animal frustration, past using his human words.

"Return her at once!" Lyssa demanded as she moved toward the army. "I demand to give her medical attention."

Kirill swore, forced to release his hold on Roderic to grab hold of his wife.

"Stop them!" Tori cried.

Other screams and demands were lost in the commotion.

"Secure our standing," the general ordered.

Suddenly, every soldier raised a weapon in unison to point them at the queen.

"No!" Kirill thrust himself in front of his wife, arms spread wide.

Roderic's body tore through his clothing as he shifted fully into a cat. Snarling, he readied his claws for the fight.

Sever jerked Justina in front of him and held a blaster pistol against her temple. Blood trickled

MICHELLE M. PILLOW

down the side of her face. She didn't resist as her arms hung limp, and her dazed expression refused to focus on any one thing.

"Roderic." Falke's voice was firm. "Don't. They'll kill her."

Roderic breathed heavily, staring at the weapon next to Justina's head. He didn't know if his uncle meant Justina or the queen, but it didn't matter. The threat to the women was about the only thing that could have kept his cougar from attacking.

The general stood, smiling, his eyes cold. He hadn't drawn a weapon, as if he knew he wouldn't be touched.

"Let this be notice of her arrest," General Sten bellowed. "She'll be afforded the same privileges as all prisoners."

Kirill backed up, pushing his wife back as he continued to shield her.

"We got what we came for." General Sten took several steps back toward the land crafts.

Sever held Justina across her shoulders and dragged her with him. She stumbled, and he lifted her in small hops to keep her on her feet. They were protected by the shield of bodies, swallowed into their ranks.

Roderic roared his disapproval, pawing at the

ground. The sound startled a few of the soldiers, and they jerked back. He breathed heavily, staring at Justina as she was hauled into a land craft and dropped onto the floor. The way he felt, he could have torn through that entire army with bare claws, but they would have fired back with weapons.

Soldiers kept their weapons trained as they backed away. The shifters didn't move as the army retreated onto their land crafts and into the forest.

"We should have never trusted them," Lyssa said as Kirill dropped his arms.

"Roderic?" His mother approached slowly, her hands outstretched and steady. He growled his frustration, but it didn't frighten her as she touched his head. She stroked his fur. "Talk to me. You need to talk to me."

"Everyone inside," Falke ordered. "We'll track their movements and do a sweep of the forest to make sure none remain behind."

His mother's hand stayed on his head, stroking his hair as he forced the animal back inside. His physical being might have changed, but the primal instinct to hunt and kill remained.

"Why was she out here?" Roderic demanded, shaking off his mother's hand as he stood. A dark abyss of anger and pain tried to fill him.

Fiora's prediction whispered through his thoughts. *"Your timeline is full of too much pain and heartache..."*

"She only tried to help," Roderic yelled in frustration, his limbs shaking with rage. "She needed our protection. I promised to protect her." He confronted the king. "How could you return her to them? You've seen her health scans. You know what kind of people they are."

"What I know and what we can prove are two different things." Kirill narrowed his eyes, but he didn't raise his voice. "The decision to return was Justina's. You did not life mate her, so you had no say in her decision to—"

"But I did!" Roderic exclaimed.

Tori gasped. "But she said..."

"Or I was going to," Roderic finished. "She didn't know. Not really. She was worried about what it would mean for me if I lost her. We were talking about it. I love her. That's what I know. I love her like she's a piece of myself. What you call it doesn't matter. I love her. I promised to protect her."

"Inside," Falke said, corralling them toward the door. "They may be listening."

The others made their way inside into the hall.

Roderic stared into the forest where the land craft disappeared.

"Are you going to stand there bemoaning the situation, or are you going to come inside so we can do something about it?" Falke demanded. "She's a brave woman. She chose to turn herself over to stop the escalation into war."

"You shouldn't have let her leave." Roderic pushed past his uncle and strode inside, stepping over his ripped clothing on the ground.

19

"Justina didn't want you to stop her. She said you know how she feels and that she needed to check on Starrs. She said you'd understand." Nadja stood in the entryway to the open laboratory, waiting for one of her processes to finish.

Roderic paced the length of his parent's home, ignoring his mother's entreaties to sit. "What I don't understand is how you all could let her."

"She's not our prisoner," his mother stated. She sat next to Lyssa and Rigan.

Roderic wondered if they thought having the women talk to him would keep his temper down. If so, it was a reasonable assumption. He was less inclined to fight with them than his uncles and King

Ualan. His father was still trapped dealing with the ambassadors. It was possible he didn't yet know.

Roderic closed his eyes and took a deep breath. "I should have stopped them. I should've saved her."

"They would've killed me, and they would have killed Justina." Lyssa folded her hands on her lap and leaned forward. "You know us well enough to know that none of us wanted this. I honestly believed she would be safe. Regardless of how she came to us, HIA and ESC intergalactic regulations give us the right to continue her medical care unless Justina tells us she doesn't want our help. The Federation Military agreed to these regulations. General Sten has to comply."

"Even if she is a prisoner?" Rigan asked. "That doesn't change things?"

"Yes. Even if she is a prisoner." Lyssa looked Roderic in the eye. Her tone had an edge to it, as if she needed the words to be drilled past his anger into his brain. "Their stating she did something wrong is not the same as them proving that list of charges against her. From what you told me, that man Sever escorted her from the facility. Even if they lie and say she ran, they won't have evidence of her stealing anything."

"Attempted distribution of unsanctioned food," Roderic said. "They're accusing her of bringing our food simulators to the city. I'll tell them I did it. Alone."

"Public disruption in a place like Shelter City is a nonsense charge," Tori said. "And damage to census drones? Who hasn't wanted to blast a few of those things out of the sky once or twice in their lives?"

"The general reminds me a lot of my father and his Medical Mafia cronies. They have so much power, so many corrupt friends, that they truly believe nothing and no one can touch them. I think even as he laid dying, my father didn't believe it was the end." Nadja frowned as if caught in a memory. "And after seeing the stunt the general pulled today, there is one thing I'm convinced of, now more than ever."

"What?" Rigan asked.

"The key to ending General Sten's reign is right here in this lab." Nadja pointed behind her.

"How can you be sure?" Roderic walked toward the laboratory as if he could somehow divine an answer from the scientific equipment.

"Buried in that list of nonsense—public disturbances and a cache of food simulators no one in Shelter City could afford—lies what they are terrified of people finding out." Nadja chose her words carefully as if still processing her thoughts. "Theft of scientific food stores for testing purposes, theft of medical property, and attempted treason. They know if we have that food and that vial, and we figure out what those strange components are, they're going to need to cover their asses. If she stole the food and the vial, and they weren't meant for distribution, then the Federation did nothing wrong. They'll say they were testing anything and everything to find a cure for the Cysgodians. They'll say she was working with us to frame the Federation for wrongdoing."

"It is no secret that we don't want them on this planet," Rigan added. "We have turned down their Alliance and *galaxa-promethium* ore mining contracts for centuries. How many times have we petitioned the Federation to remove the base and let the Cysgodian people decide for themselves?"

"And then General Sten will be able to make a case for staying permanently on Qurilixen," Roderic concluded.

"Sten will make us look deceitful, and he'll be some great victor fighting for the little people against the tyranny of a shifter planet that wanted control over the Cysgodians," Rigan concluded. "If I'm a reporter on the outside looking in, that's a story to sell newspaper chips. It's a story I would have sold to my editor Gus at *The Universal* back in the day. It sure beats the soft, romantic piece about alien princes looking for brides he sent me here to write a lifetime ago. I think we sometimes forget, being so isolated in the Y quadrant, but public perception is half the battle. If Sten tells that story, people all across the universes will cheer the Federation for putting us in our place."

"Then maybe it's time you wrote a different narrative," Nadja said.

Rigan furrowed her brow.

"I'm serious. If they want to fight, then we must attack them on all fronts," Nadja said.

"I agree." Lyssa stood and began to pace. "Rigan, write it. Tell everyone across the universes how the Cysgodians are being treated. We finally have evidence with Justina's scans. As soon as we're done analyzing the samples, you'll have almost everything you need for a story, and we'll be able to use that to force our way into the city to test more people. Once we have enough proof, you should contact anyone from *The Universal* who will listen. If they don't, we'll call Jarek and Reid back and make them fly us to the newspaper chip headquarters."

"I'll have Grier fly over the city again wearing my old eye camera," Rigan said. "The living conditions alone aren't enough, or we would've done it already, but it's very damning with this new information. We'll be able to compare the footage with the images we took when they first arrived."

"And I'll send everything to the HIA," Lyssa said. "They're always in a pissing contest with the Federation Military."

"And to my colleagues at ESC," Tori added. "I'll request a ship to help process the population. General Sten may call us primitive scientists on Qurilixen, but I'd like to see him try to use that excuse with the Exploratory Science Commission."

"Sacred cats, you women are a little terrifying," Roderic said, in awe of how fast they formulated their plan.

"Men tend to think of fighting as using fang and claws," Tori said.

"Or talon," Rigan added.

"Right, and talon," Tori agreed.

"But there are many ways to win an argument," Nadja said. A small beep sounded, and she turned to walk inside the lab to check the progress.

Tori went to her son. She touched his face gently. "But there is a place for claws and talons in the world as well. Get Jaxx, Fiora, Grier, and Payton. You know the city better than anyone. Go figure out a way to rescue my future daughter."

20

JUSTINA HATED DARKNESS, BUT THERE WAS something to be said for time being marked by night. The constant daylight of Qurilixen became an endless crawling of moments until she could no longer track how many hours or days had passed hanging in the middle of Shelter City by her cuffed hands, bound and gagged, a chilling example of what it meant to defy the Federation's rule.

Justina had been there long enough that the gathered crowd had parted, and the city flowed around her. At first, the soldiers had been stationed at her posts to yell warnings about helping her down, but as the onlookers left, so had they. She had become a fixture, no more important than a piece of canvas flapping in the breeze trapped between two posts. Now drones flew by to check on her.

This punishment was worse than a tiny white cell with no windows.

"Do you think they care about you?" General Sten had whispered in her ear as they prepared her punishment. His cruel eyes took delight in her fear. *"In your pretty new dress, stinking of shifters? Do you think any of them will thank you for what you did when I cut their rations? I'll make sure they know who's to blame. Every one of them will come by to see your pretty face. And then, when I let you down and lock you in your home, well, your friends and their humanitarian medical regulations won't matter if you're murdered by your own. Do you think anyone will help the shifters after they hear about your fate?"*

Justina had underestimated the general. She had genuinely believed that she would have been safe to return with the backing of the shifters and intergalactic sanctions.

And she never said goodbye to Roderic.

Thinking of him was almost too painful to bear, a true heartache, but his face kept surfacing in her mind as she relived each moment. All she wanted was one chance to say she loved him and that she wished more than anything they could have been written into the same story.

Perhaps if they were given a next life. Cysgodians didn't believe in that, but maybe.

There was one person who would help her. She'd seen Starrs lingering in the background as if considering how to get past the guards. Thankfully, he hadn't tried, or he would have been strung up next to her.

Her feet dangled a foot off the ground, tied together so she couldn't fight off the children who ran under the gallows to swing her back and forth like a pendulum. She cried out against her gag, the muffled anger turning to pleas for them to stop.

A particularly sprightly lad with tangled brown hair ran and leaped at her, grabbing hold of her legs to hold on as he swung. The extra weight jarred both shoulders and cut the cuffs into her wrists. Blood trailed down her arms. The child's laughter rang out to complete the torment, joined by a few watching adults.

General Sten was right. No one would help her.

"Off!" Starrs appeared from the crowd, swinging a pole like a sword. The children screamed and scurried away. The boy slid off her legs and gave her one last push before he ran after his friends.

Tears slid down her cheeks from the pain. Starrs dropped his pole and caught her. He lifted her up to sit on his shoulder, taking the pressure off her arms. She sighed in relief at the reprieve, even as her body throbbed with pain. Blood dripped off her elbow and dotted his shirt.

Starrs looked up at her, twisting slightly. "You. Down."

Justina gave a slight moan against the gag and shook her head. She did not want the Federation making an example out of Starrs for helping her.

"Run." Starrs held her steady.

Justina dropped her head against her arm and breathed heavily. Her feet tingled. Even if she found secure footing, she couldn't have stood, let alone run.

Starrs shook her to get her attention. "Run."

Justina looked up at her hands. The cuffs were latched onto the gallows. She shook her wrists, seeing if she could find a way to free them.

The buzz of drones caught her attention as three armed units came from the sky to surround them.

"*Mm-mum!*" Justina reached her hands wide. She tried to wiggle free from Starr's hold. She swung her legs, kicking him lightly to get him to drop her.

"Run!" Starrs screamed, holding her tighter.

The lights on the drones changed color.

Onlookers ran for cover. Justina closed her eyes tight and braced for impact. The drones gave a high-pitched whine of warning.

Suddenly a roar rang out, followed by the sound of running feet pounding the dirt. She opened her eyes to a blur of movement coming at them. Roderic and Jaxx rammed themselves against the gallows poles. Her body jerked. She screamed in surprise as her hands were pulled backward. Starrs caught her on the way down, blocking her fall with his body as she landed on top of him.

Grier appeared a few paces behind them, completely naked. He leaped into the air. His body burst into the form of a dragon as his talons crushed two of the drones. They snapped and popped under his grip. The last one tried to evade the dragon, and Grier spouted fire at it. A flaming ball of burning metal shot across the sky and crashed into the side of the cliff. Screams could be heard all around the city as the drone exploded.

Roderic appeared over her with a handheld laser cutter. "Hold still. I'm going to cut you free."

He set to work on her wrists. A crushed drone dropped on the ground next to them, sparking its last bits of current, as Grier flew up into the sky.

"Hurry!" Jaxx yelled, darting past them.

Her cuffs broke loose from the gallows, and she rolled off Starrs. Justina pried the gag from her mouth. Roderic cut the binds around her ankles with the laser. When her legs were free, Roderic pulled her up by the arm to a sitting position. Payton and Fiora swept in with a cloak, wrapping it around Justina from behind before hauling her to her feet.

Grier flew past, spouting fire and drawing attention to himself.

Roderic swept her into his arms as he ran from the gallows. The others followed.

"Left," Fiora commanded.

They all turned down a narrow alleyway only to emerge from the other side.

"Put her down," Fiora said.

Roderic set Justina on her feet. She swayed. Her legs trembled to support her.

"Wait." Fiora huddled close to Jaxx and watched a group of people run past them. She closed her eyes and concentrated.

"You came for me," Justina whispered, gazing up at Roderic. The cuffs weighed down her arms, and she didn't try to lift them. "I'm sorry you had to come for me. I knew I'd be in trouble, but I didn't think they'd arrest me."

"I'll always come for you," Roderic swore,

pulling her wrists up by the cuffs. He began cutting her free with the laser. "Try not to move. I don't want to hurt you."

Starrs ran his hand over her head and patted her a few times. He nodded and then let her go. "Good."

"Thank you," Justina said to the others. "I know how much you're risking by helping me."

"You're family," Payton answered. "Or you will be once Roderic gets his act together."

"Payton, don't you have to see a half mate—*I mean cyborg*—about payment?" Roderic pulled the cuffs off Justina's hands, freeing her.

Payton held out her hand.

Roderic tossed the laser he'd used to cut Justina free from the gallows. Payton caught it with one hand. He threw the cuffs, and she caught them with the other.

"I'll bring these to Yevgen to settle our debt and see if he's picked up any threats we need to know about. Try not to have any fun without me." Payton disappeared between two buildings.

Roderic gently rubbed her hands, careful not to touch where the cuffs had cut her. When she gazed into his eyes, she felt as if their minds were trying to connect, as if his thoughts whispered through her mind and hers through his. Everything he felt was there for her to read in his gaze—fear, desire, hope, determination. Most importantly, it reflected her love for him and his for her.

Jaxx reached under his tunic and handed Justina a satchel. "We thought you might be hungry."

Inside were slices of blue bread with some kind of meat. She tore it into two pieces and handed half to Starrs. He nodded his thanks as they both quickly took bites.

Jaxx took a container hanging from his wife's belt and gave that to Justina as well. "Water."

Justina shared the water with her friend too. Starrs wrapped most of his food into a bundle with a scrap of material he pulled from a pocket, conserving it for later out of habit.

Grier flew past, spouting a quick succession of fireballs before letting loose a long stream.

"Soldiers are coming," Jaxx said, translating Grier's warning.

"Jaxx, I got one," Fiora stated, opening her eyes. She glanced at Justina eating as if she'd not heard what had been happening around her.

Justina started to ask what the woman meant, but Roderic asked, "Can you walk?"

Justina nodded.

Fiora and Jaxx led the way down the street. Starrs trailed behind.

Justina's thoughts cleared with the food and water. Her senses became sharper. "Where are we going?"

"Evading capture," Roderic answered. He glanced back at Starrs. "If we get separated, do what we talked about."

"Good," Starrs answered.

To Justina, he said, "If anything happens, go with Starrs."

"I'm not leaving you," she protested.

Grier whooshed past, dipping low to scatter the crowd out of the street. He turned in the air, dive-bombing the opening he'd made on the ground. Right before impact, he shifted and rolled into his human form.

Fiora pulled the cloak from her shoulders and tossed it at Grier, who swung it over his body to hide his nakedness.

"Hurry!" Grier demanded. "We're going to miss our chance."

Grier ran through the streets. People gasped, jumping out of his way.

"Roderic," Justina pulled at his arm. "They saw him land. They'll know shifters are in the city."

"Trust me." Roderic cupped her cheek and gave her a light kiss.

She nodded. "Yes."

They made their way through the streets. The flow of the crowd changed. Instead of running from them, the Cysgodians began to stampede toward them. The sound of blaster pistols heightened their panic. She saw a line of black uniforms coming down the side of the cliff from the facility in the distance. Drones swarmed like insects over their heads, spreading out through the sky.

Terrified screams came from every direction. Roderic held her hand tight, weaving through the thickening crowd. Someone knocked against her, pushing her aside. Her grasp slipped from Roderic's hold, and she fell to the ground. A heavy boot stepped on her hand, and another kicked her leg. Justina cried out in pain.

Arms wrapped around her waist seconds later and lifted her from danger.

"Starrs?" Roderick yelled. "Starrs!"

"Good!" Starrs hollered. He lifted Justina over his shoulder and pushed forward, bracing her with one hand and shoving his palm to knock people out of his way with the other.

"Now!" Fiora screamed.

Starrs dropped her on her feet and hunched over her, shielding her with his body. A loud explosion lit up the street, blasting heat as bits of metal and stone rained down on them.

Roderic appeared next to them. He pulled Justina to her feet. "Well done, Starrs."

"Good," Starrs answered.

A building to her right burned brightly.

"Get the children to safety!" a man yelled.

"There is no place safe!" a terrified voice answered.

Words were lost in a chaos of shouting and running feet.

"Get back into your homes," a steady voice boomed over the rest, amplified by a drone flying overhead. It echoed from different parts of the city. "Anyone rioting on the streets will be shot."

"Where are our rations?" Maler, a man Justina had watched cart rocks through the streets for decades, appeared from near the fire. He drew back his arm and launched a rock at the drone, smacking it on the side. Cheers went up from those who witnessed the attack. The unit clanked before flying in sporadic angles. Its speaker system became distorted, popping out incomprehensible words. Maler aimed another stone, hitting it a second time. The unit went down.

"You!" Maler pointed at her with a firm nod. "We're with you!"

Justina blinked in confusion.

"Fight, fight, fight," Maler chanted, clutching a rock as he pumped his fist. "Take them all down!"

Others joined the battle cry as they took off down the street.

"To the end!" a woman shouted, wielding a piece of jagged metal like a knife. A portion of her dress had been wrapped around the end to create a hilt.

"To the bloody end!" another woman shouted, her hoarse voice full of decades of building rage.

"What's happening?" Justina asked in disbelief.

"You were right. Given a chance, the Cysgodians would fight," Roderic answered. "All they needed was to know they had our backing."

Federation soldiers marched toward them. Roderic's hand shifted beneath hers as he became half man, half cat.

"Get back into your homes," a soldier ordered, only to be tackled by three men before he could lift a weapon.

"Fire!" a commander ordered. Blasts shot out at the crowd, deflecting on metal shields.

Fiora appeared at Justina's side. Jaxx and Grier jumped up, transforming and taking to flight. Soldiers fired on them, but their dragon bodies absorbed the blasts. They breathed flames down onto their heads, scattering the soldiers. Suddenly, more dragons appeared in the sky, swooping in to overtake the drones.

Cat-shifters burst through the streets next to dragon-men. All the shifters moved with supernatural speed. She'd never seen the dragons in half-human form. Hardened brown skin covered their bodies. Yellow eyes seemed to glow. Hard tissue covered their foreheads and nose, creating a battering ram with which they head-butted the enemy while wielding their taloned fingers with devastating results. Blades and blasters didn't slow them and seemed to glance off their bodies, leaving them unharmed.

The cats were just as fierce, moving with predatory grace, mauling and sprinting at incredible speeds. They dodged the blasters. Claws swiped the enemy before they could fire a second time.

Seeing a woman on the ground, arms raised to block a strike from a soldier, Justina charged the man and knocked him over. Before she could find her footing, Roderic was there. He held out his hand to help the woman to her feet. She stared at the clawed appendage before slowly taking it. As she let go of him, she nodded and rejoined the fight.

Shadows cast over them as the dragons flew above. They hurled the drones like missiles at the facility.

"Surrender." The first cry was soft, coming from the distance but was soon repeated.

Soldiers dropped their weapons, lifting their hands into the air and falling to their knees for mercy. The fallen from both sides littered the streets.

Fiora climbed to the top of a rubbish pile and lifted her arms. Jaxx swooped in from above and dropped a bundle. She caught it and instantly tore it open to reveal several devices.

"Roderic!" Fiora threw one at him. He caught it and ran to kneel by a man holding his stomach.

"Justina, help," Fiora said, tossing a small device at her.

Justina barely managed to catch it as she cradled her crushed fingers.

Fiora held up a matching unit and demonstrated its use on Justina's hand. "Handheld medic. Hold it over the worst wounds. Push this button. It will do the rest."

Justina nodded. As the unit worked, the pain in her hand went away, and the bruises faded.

The chaos of the fight soon moved into the disarray of the aftermath. Starrs helped move rubble to pull people from a collapsed building. Justina, Roderic, and Fiora moved from body to body, offering medical care. Soldiers and Cysgodians, it didn't matter. If they needed help, they received it.

Justina barely had time to register the full implications of what had happened. Federation soldiers were taken into custody by the Draig and Var.

Drones reappeared overhead. A new voice sounded over the speakers, and Justina recognized Queen Lyssa repeating the message, "We have food. We have medical. We have decontaminators. Please stay in the city. Everyone will be helped. We have food. We have medical .."

Cheering roared over the city, filling the valley. The air had become lighter, as if those shouts somehow expelled decades of frustration.

"Come on." Jaxx appeared with Fiora with a piece of canvas wrapped around his waist.

Roderic kept her close. She felt their connection growing. Justina waved at Starrs to join them. He shook his head and continued helping clean up the rubble.

They crossed through the city and climbed up the side of the cliff. Cats and dragons moved with precision, walking prisoners to temporary holding cells. She saw Sever in one of the lines. The man refused to look up from the ground.

On the top of the cliff, the royal elders waited for them. Smoke rose from within the facility. The entryway had been scorched.

Falke had taken the general into custody and the evil man sat in a cage. "By authorization of the humanitarian accord enacted between HIA, ESC, and the Federation, for the prosecution of planetary genocidal acts, I hereby detain you for trial."

Upon seeing them, Tori ran to her son. She hugged Roderic and then Justina. "Thank the gods you're safe."

"How...?" Justina looked at the general, unable to believe her own eyes. She'd dreamed of such a thing but never thought she'd see it.

"It's all thanks to what you gave us. Your blood proves the blue radiation is safe, as are the food simulators, decontaminators, and medical booths. It is the food rations that have been hurting you. They're tainted with a hazardous material. That is why you—and I suspect most of the population—had so many masses growing inside you," Tori answered.

Nadja joined them. "The vial of black liquid was an aggression agent. It would give vitamins and energy while making their victim angry. They wanted the city to become discontent, unmanageable, and for it to fall into more chaos than there already is."

"Look for the one we call Yellow Shirt," Fiora said to Tori. "I finally saw into the bag he received as payment for the food simulator. You'll find several vials among various items for trade. Proof that they did distribute their poison into the city. If you put pressure on him, he'll tell you everything. I've found other vials too. We need to encourage everyone to turn them over when they get their medical scans."

Justina stared at the general. His cold eyes peered back at her.

"Justina, are you all right?" Roderic asked, drawing her attention away from the wicked man.

"He was trying to kill us all," Justina whispered, leaning into his arms. "Why? What did he have to gain by it?"

"I don't know," Roderic answered. "But you're safe now. That's what matters."

"The dragon princes are on the other side of the valley. They helped coordinate the attacks," Tori said. "Fiora's visions told us the Federation would go after the city at the first hint of rebellion, and we wanted to make that battle as short as possible."

One of the cat-shifters leaped over the side of the cliff from below, fur rippling into naked human flesh as he came forward. "One of the prisoners is trying to make a deal. Information for leniency."

"Who?" Kirill inquired.

"What does he know?" Ualan asked at the same time.

"It says *Sever* on his shirt," the guard answered. "He claims to have proof of a plan to stake claim to the planet of Cysgod once it is inhabitable in a few hundred years. If there are no living descendants at that time, as the last remaining governance of the Cysgodian people, the Federation Military will be able to keep the planet on their roster permanently."

Justina had not expected to get an answer to her question so quickly. All of this torture was to take over a virus-ridden planet in a few hundred years?

"That is why they needed you to be in the city, so they can keep track of everyone." Roderic pulled Justina closer as if he could shield her from everything wrong in the universes.

"They'd blame our illness on the virus," Justina reasoned. "And if the tainted food didn't kill us fast enough, they'd drug us into killing each other. That's why they said one drop. They wanted to document a slow progression of random violence over time."

"Justina, we recognize you as the official spokesperson and first Qurilixian leader for your people. Without your bravery, they would not be free," Kirill said. "And your people will need a clear leader now more than ever as we move forward."

Ualan nodded his agreement. "It is for you to decide whether Sever receives leniency for exchange of information."

Justina looked at Roderic for his thoughts.

"Whatever you decide, Queen Justina," Roderic said. "We trust you."

"No. Not yet," she decided. "First, we should see what we can find out from the facility and question my people. No one should be set free if they had a hand in this."

"Sound judgment." Kirill nodded.

"Spoken like a true royal," Ualan added.

"And maybe just Lady Justina, not Queen," she suggested. "It seems strange declaring myself a queen without my people having a say."

"As you wish, my lady," Roderic answered.

"Some of the citizens have taken to the forest," Prince Quinn informed them. "We should send men after them to bring them back. They might not know they need medical care, and the danger has passed."

Kirill and Ualan joined Quinn as they went to tell Falke.

"Look at that." Fiora stood at the cliffside and waved her hand over the view of the city. Trails of smoke came from several locations. Cheers of celebration resounded like a strange song. "It worked. It all worked." Fiora grinned and turned to Justina. "Oh, and the people are going to vote for you to be their queen. So you might as well get used to the title."

Justina opened her mouth to speak, but nothing came out. Her? A queen?

"And Roderic—" Fiora began.

"No," Roderic held up his hand to stop her. "No more predictions."

"I was just going to tell you the heartache is over." Fiora continued grinning as she went to join Jaxx and the other dragons.

"That's not a prediction. That's something my heart already knows." Roderic wrapped his arm around Justina's shoulders, holding her back against his chest. "Look at that, my lady. Your people are now free to do what they want."

"Within reason, of course. We all have to act within reason. There will be a lot of work to do and a lot of conversations to have." Justina cupped his face in her hands and kissed him deeply. Then, nodding toward the city in the valley, she added, "I think we can safely say that those life debts you think you owe us have been paid in full. In fact, I might have to spend the rest of my life paying you back for the lives you all saved today."

"They can stay here in the city and rebuild. We can help send them to other parts of space if that's what they wish." Roderic chuckled. "There have already been several requests from the dragon bachelors to invite the single Cysgodian women to the next bridal ceremony."

Justina laughed. "That might go over much better than you think. I happen to know for a fact that shifter fantasies are prevalent among that segment of the population."

"Oh, really?" He grinned.

Justina nodded. "Really. I've had a few myself."

He turned her in his arms so that they could face each other. "And what about you, my lady? What will you do now that you are free?"

Tears of happiness wet her eyes. So much joy hardly seemed possible. "I want you to be my life mate."

Roderic grinned and leaned to kiss her. Emotion poured out of her into him until she felt she could hear his thoughts echoing inside of her. She felt his desire as if it were her own. Her heart beat in time with his. And somehow, she knew that willing it to happen had made it so. He was her husband. He belonged to her, and she belonged to him. Forever.

"I guess I was wrong," she whispered against his mouth. "Our stories were written in the same book. It just took us a while to get here. I love you, Roderic."

"And I love you, my lady." He kissed her again. The cheers continued in the city below.

Forever.

The End

MEET RODERIC'S PARENTS

Keep Reading!
Find out about Roderic's Parents

Lords of the Var®: The Playful Prince

Cat-shifter Prince Quinn isn't looking for a serious relationship. In fact, he's never even considered it. He's content to enjoy life to the fullest, never taking anything but his royal duties seriously. However, when a new scientist arrives to test for biological weapons, he can't seem to stay away from her.

Dr. Tori Elliot is at the palace to do a job and no matter what she's going to act like a professional... which means not succumbing to the seductively sexy playful prince.

.

THE SERIES CONTINUES...

Need more Dragon Lords?

Dragon Lords: Barbarian Prince

What more Cat-Shifters?

Lords of the Var®: The Savage King

**Dragon Lords and *Lords of the Var*®
in Modern Day Earth?**

Captured by a Dragon-Shifter: Determined Prince

**Read all the Dragon Lords and Var books?
Yay, you, keep going!**

Space Lords: His Frost Maiden

WELCOME TO QURILIXEN

QURILIXEN WORLD - FIRST IN SERIES BOOKS

Keep Reading!
Check out these first-in-series books in the different Qurilixen World series installments!

The Qurilixen World is an extensive collection of science fiction and paranormal romance novels by award-winning NYT Bestselling author, *Michelle M. Pillow*®. Note: Each book in each series is a stand alone story.

Dragon Lords Series: Barbarian Prince

Dragon Shapeshifter Romance - The original Dragon Lords series' Anniversary Edition

Going undercover at a mass wedding as a bartered bride, Morrigan Blake has every intention of getting off the barbaric alien planet just as soon as the ceremony over. But the next morning, Morrigan discovers her ride left without her and an alien dragon shifter is claiming she's his wife. It's not exactly the story this reporter had in mind. And to make matters worse, the all-to-seductive dragon-shifter alpha male refuses to take no for an answer.

Lords of the Var® Series: The Savage King
Cat-Shifter Romance

Cat-shifting King Kirill knows he must do his royal duty by his people. When his father unexpectedly dies, it's his destiny to take the throne and all of the responsibility that entails. What he hadn't prepared for is the troublesome prisoner that's now his to deal with.

Undercover Agent Ulyssa is no man's captive. Trapped in a primitive alien forest awaiting pickup, she's going to make the best out of a bad situation... which doesn't include falling for the seductions of an alpha male king.

Dynasty Lords Series: Seduction of the Phoenix

Science Fiction Romance

A prince raised in honor and tradition, a woman raised with nothing at all. She wants to steal their most sacred treasure. He'll do anything to protect it, even if it means marrying a thief.

Space Lords Series: His Frost Maiden

Science Fiction Space Pirate Romance

Lady Josselyn of the House of Craven has been betrayed. With her home world on a Florencian moon under attack and her family dead, she finds herself at the mercy of the one who deceived them. There is only one thing left to do—die with honor. But before she can join her family in the afterlife, she must first avenge all that she held dear. Falling in love with a pirate was never in the plan. Evan and his thieving crewmates might have delayed her fate, but they can't stop destiny.

Captured by a Dragon-Shifter Series: Determined Prince
Dragon Shapeshifter Romance

Dragon-shifter Prince Kyran has studied the Earth people and is ready to assimilate. Female shifters are all but going extinct on his planet of Qurilixen, and his people are desperate for mates—so much so they're taking matters into their own hands. What better place to find a mate than Earth? After all, dragon-shifters had come from there centuries ago. Surely a human female would be honored to be selected by one as fine and fierce as himself.

Galaxy Alien Mail Order Brides: Spark

Alien Romance

Earth women better watch out. Things are about to heat up.

Mining ash on a remote planet where temperatures reach hellish degrees doesn't leave Kal (aka Spark) much room for dating. Lucky for this hardworking man, a new corporation Galaxy Alien Mail Order Brides is ready to help him find the girl of his dreams. Does it really matter that he lied on his application and really isn't looking for long term, but rather some fast action? Earth women better watch out. Things are about to heat up.

Happy Reading!

MichellePillow.com

ABOUT MICHELLE M. PILLOW

New York Times & *USA TODAY* Bestselling Author

Michelle loves to travel and try new things, whether it's a paranormal investigation of an old Vaudeville Theatre or climbing Mayan temples in Belize. She believes life is an adventure fueled by copious amounts of coffee.

Newly relocated to the American South, Michelle is involved in various film and documentary projects with her talented director husband. She is mom to a fantastic artist. And she's managed by a dog and cat who make sure she's meeting her deadlines.

For the most part she can be found wearing pajama pants and working in her office. There may or may not be dancing. It's all part of the creative process.

Come say hello! Michelle loves talking with readers on social media!

www.MichellePillow.com

facebook.com/AuthorMichellePillow

x.com/michellepillow

instagram.com/michellempillow

bookbub.com/authors/michelle-m-pillow

goodreads.com/Michelle_Pillow

amazon.com/author/michellepillow

youtube.com/michellepillow

pinterest.com/michellepillow

JOIN THE EXCLUSIVE CLUB!

Join the Pillow Fighters' Reader Club to stay informed about new books, sales, contests, giveaways, exclusive content, preorders and more!

michellepillow.com/author-updates

Readers who love this series,
love the *Warlocks MacGregors*®!

Spirits and Spells
By Michelle M. Pillow

Niall MacGregor, a Scottish werewolf, used magic to steal Charlotte Carver's memories to protect her. But as she begins to remember little things and their sizzling passion heats up, will temptation bring her closer to the truth?

Magick, Mischief & Kilts!
Charlotte Carver is going insane—suffering

everything from memory loss to hallucinations, to phantom conversations she can't recall having. Something tells her it's not a coincidence that it all started when the MacGregor family moved to town, and the one person who knows what's going on is the last person Charlotte would ask for help. Her new landlord, Niall MacGregor, is not the most approachable man but that hasn't stopped the brooding Scottish biker from invading her dreams.

When Charlotte's memories start to return, she's not sure she can trust what they are telling her. If magic does exist, then is her attraction to Niall just an illusion?

Motorcycle riding werewolf, Niall MacGregor is the longtime supernatural enforcer for his warlock family. He has regretted more than a few things that he's done in the name of duty, but taking Charlotte's memories ranks as one of the worst. It was necessary, to both protect his magical family and save Charlotte's sanity. But the intimate glimpse into her mind has only made him want things he can never have— including the love of the gorgeous, brave woman herself.

Something from Niall's past has come back to threaten everything he holds dear.

Warning: Contains yummy, hot, mischievous MacGregors who are almost certainly up to no good on their quest to find true love. And Uncle Raibeart.

PLEASE LEAVE A REVIEW

THANK YOU FOR READING!

Please take a moment to share your thoughts by reviewing this book.

Be sure to check out Michelle's other titles at

www.MichellePillow.com